SUE BIRCH

DEAD PUZZLING

This book is dedicated to my three wonderful sons Mike, Tim and Ben because without them Oliver would not have been born. Also my nephew David for without him Oliver's story would not have been told. And, of course, the National Autistic Society for without them Oliver's story would not have had the same ending.

Contents

1. Some*body*'s in the graveyard
2. The detectives
3. What a wondrous web we weave
4. Ironing out problems
5. Things start to heat up
6. The butcher of Allsworthy
7. Oliver does a vanishing trick
8. Oliver's made plans
9. Oliver's not so clueless
10. The library holds a story
11. An instrument of torture
12. Stranger and stranger
13. The great escape
14. A watery grave
15; Oliver's got a complaint
16. The long arm of the criminal
17. Back to school
18. In at the deep end

Chapter one.

Somebody's in the graveyard.

"Darn it! I'd lose me 'ead if it weren't screwed on tight!" Harry wheezed through gaps where teeth should have been as he searched amongst the graves. Peering round a headstone his watery old eyes caught sight of an urn that was leaning over about to fall off its base.

He set it straight with his gnarled, soil-grimed fingers before scratching at the last two hairs clinging to the top of his head. The puzzled look returned, adding more wrinkles to his already prune like face, as Harry tried to remember where he'd left the shears he'd been gardening with half an hour earlier.

He shrugged his shoulders knowing that although the memory was gone the shears would no doubt return. Tugging a handful of weeds out of the green chippings covering Granny Grant's final resting place he tossed them into his rusty wheelbarrow before hobbling off along the neatly trimmed path.

Despite being the oldest gravedigger in Britain Harry took pride in looking after his residents. He kept their grass cut, their headstones moss free and made it a point to know the name, age and plot number of each of his tenants as well as the face of almost every regular visitor the churchyard received.

As he turned down by the ancient yew Harry froze mid shuffle dropping the handles of his barrow. Only the hunch on his stooped back prevented him from standing up straight in surprise.

He did not know this visitor to his graveyard. He didn't know the name or recognize the face that was twisted round staring in shocked surprise towards him. And Harry didn't know why the man should be sprawled across Mr. Price's grave with the lost shears sticking out of his back!

Harry ran to Allsworthy vicarage as fast as his old legs allowed him.

Oliver tottered round Allsworthy School changing rooms as fast as his boots allowed him shouting at his teacher, "I won't! I won't! I won't!"

Mr. Jones snorted with rage and glared at the fair-haired boy before bellowing, "What are you? You're a big girl's blouse that's what you are!"

Lizzie knew that when he was younger and still had hair Mr. Jones wanted to play rugby for his country. But his wishes hadn't come true so he'd turned to teaching to help other youngsters reach their goals. He often pointed out to the pupils that a boy wasn't a "proper" boy unless he was sporty.

Oliver looked like any other nine year old lad but although his hair was cropped short in the latest style and he wore Nike tee shirt and trainers he didn't like sport.

Lizzie could tell by his twitching eyelid that Oliver's refusal to join the game of football outside was making the teacher very cross.

"I don't want to play football," Oliver, his pale skin turning white with fear and anger yelled back at Mr. Jones.

"Every time I play games I get tripped up, knocked over or shouted at! The ball hit me in the face last week! Twice! It hurt! Besides," he pointed to his feet. "I can't wear these. It's like wearing stilts!" Oliver could not get used to the studs on the bottom of football boots.

Teetering over to a wooden bench he sat down under hooks where shirts and jumpers hung with their sleeves pulled inside out. Tugging off the boots he flung them onto the floor in disgust shouting, "They don't work. Somebody must have broken them!"

The man thrust his red face towards Oliver's just as Mrs. Williams the head teacher walked in. Like Lizzie she'd also been sent for to "deal with Oliver".

Mrs. Williams took Mr. Jones to one side at the same time nodding to Lizzie to sit down on the bench. As she did so Oliver shuffled away from her.

Looking in the changing room mirror Lizzie could see why they were often mistaken for twins. Although her fair hair was much longer than Oliver's they did look alike. But at eleven years old Lizzie Pickles was two years older than her brother.

Lizzie glanced towards the team of lads who were crowding round the doorway straining to hear what Mrs. Williams had to say. But she spoke so softly as she peered over her glasses that no one could make out a word. Mr. Jones was looking at a dead fly squashed on the wall above her dark, curly hair.

Lizzie slid along the bench towards her brother whose legs swung beneath him as he stared at a piece of chewing gum stuck to the changing room floor.

"Oliver you mustn't be rude to Mr. Jones," she said. "If he tells you to go outside you've got to go. You'll get into trouble otherwise. You don't want that do you? You don't want them to send for Mum again? Be good okay?"

Oliver shrugged his shoulders then nodded.

By the time Lizzie got up to leave Mrs. Williams had already gone back to her office.

Mr. Jones bit on his bottom lip trying to stop it from joining his eyelid in twitching. "Right then," he said. "Let's be 'aving you outside, shall we? No more of this nonsense, eh?"

Oliver stared at him for a full minute before replying, "I'll go outside. But I won't play football. I'll read."

All the children jumped as Mr. Jones punched the wall he was leaning against so hard that a cabinet above his head shifted from its bracket. The contents of silver cups and wooden plaques shot against its glass doors and showered Mr. Jones with a torrent of silver ware and razor sharp shards of wood and glass. As the audience of waiting students gasped Lizzie heard Oliver mutter, "Temper, temper."

*

Back in her classroom on the first floor Lizzie watched from the window as the footballers trooped to the school playing field. She saw the teacher wave Oliver over to the edge of the football pitch next to the staff car park. Her brother opened a book and read for a few seconds. Then he twisted and squirmed changing his position several times. Lizzie felt sure the heat of the summer sun was making it difficult for him to focus on the story he was reading. She knew even the smell of the tarmac would be enough to upset him. As he fidgeted Oliver looked towards the vehicles parked close by. Lizzie wondered if he too could see the shimmering rays of heat rising from their bonnets.

Oliver told Lizzie later there was no particular reason he had such a beautiful and unselfish thought. He just decided the gleaming, sleek, silver animal that he had seen should really be in their mum's collection of pottery pets which juggled for space on the mantelpiece at home.

Their dad wasn't very good at choosing presents and every Christmas or birthday he gave his wife the same thing, an ornament. It had started with a china cow now she had a dog, a duck, a donkey, a tortoise, a monkey, an elephant, even a duck billed platypus. But she did not have anything as lovely as this.

The P.E. teacher's voice carried through Lizzie's open first floor window. She turned to watch looking down on the top of the man's bald head which was ripening like a tomato in the hot sun. Mr. Jones's tummy struggled to get out of the navy-blue tracksuit as he jogged up and down shouting advice to one of the slower lads.

"What's the matter with you? Your legs broken? Run boy run! Move your backside you lazy little toe-rag!"

Looking back to Oliver Lizzie saw him grasp a small statue that was on the front of a car and wriggle it as if trying to work it free. Then using two hands and placing one foot on the bumper he wrenched harder. Next he looked around and Lizzie watched as he fetched a rope that was hanging out of the sport's equipment box. Looping one end over the leaping feline on the car's bonnet he pulled on the other. He tugged and yanked with all his strength. But as far as Lizzie could tell it was no use. It looked as if the figurine had held on tight and was not budging.

Lizzie was about to put up her hand and ask to go down to the car park when Oliver seemed to lose interest in the creature. She stayed in her seat not wanting to draw more attention to her brother's behaviour.

She watched Oliver walk over to a young cherry tree the cord still hanging limply from his hand. He circled the trunk as if in a trance gazing down at the snake like pattern the coils of rope made as he went round and round. He tucked one end into a loop on the ground then grabbed his book and sat down in the shade of the tree.

Heaving a sigh of relief Lizzie turned back to her French lesson.

When the twelve o'clock bell rang for lunch neither she nor Mr. Jones noticed the missing rope and Oliver did not remember he had removed it from the box.

*

The rope stayed forgotten until lunchtime. Lizzie, munching on an apple in the playground, watched Mrs. Williams back out of her parking space with a tree chasing after her.

The girl gaped in horror as the head teacher slammed on her brakes and screeched to a halt but the tree continued its journey. Lizzie heard the sound of breaking glass and twisting metal and then a new noise like pebbles raining down on the roof of the teacher's once luxurious car.

Peering through the steam rising from under the bonnet Lizzie saw the look of shocked surprise on the head teacher's face as a final cherry bounced onto her cracked windscreen. It rolled down the glass before coming to rest next to the silver jaguar that was still firmly attached to the front of the vehicle.

Lizzie, Mr. Jones, dozens of pupils and several dinner ladies ran over to inspect the damage just as a white police car swung through the school gates. Lizzie's stomach knotted in fear at the thought of the trouble her brother may be in.

"How did they hear about this so quickly?" Mrs. Williams groaned as she climbed out of her car. "I don't think it's a police matter." Looking back at the mess she sighed, "I would like to know how it happened though."

Mr. Jones nodded in Lizzie's direction and spat out just two words, "Oliver Pickles."

"Ah! Oliver." Mrs. Williams shook her head and sighed again. "I'm afraid we're going to have to watch that boy very closely."

"We said that last time when he put the hamster down the toilet to see if it could swim," Mr. Jones said as he watched a large policeman come running over towards them.

But the policeman was not there because of Oliver. "Call the parents!" he panted gasping for breath. "We're shutting the school! There's been a murder!"

Chapter two.

The detectives.

The head teacher's car was of no interest once the murder was announced. All the villagers including Mrs. Dale, who was the postmistress, shopkeeper and village gossip, wanted to know who the poor man was and why he had been killed in Allsworthy village churchyard.

Lizzie Pickles, her brother Oliver and her best friend Tom White wanted to know too. The idea that someone had been stabbed to death on their own doorstep terrified and fascinated them. But they would not hide under the bedclothes like other children. They wanted to find out who was the village killer. With the school shut early and the extra long summer holidays stretching ahead Lizzie, Oliver and Tom, who had always wanted to be a detective, decided they would solve the crime.

Lizzie who was nicknamed the "Helpful Elf" by her mother always looked after Oliver. She reminded him to pick up his coat as he left for school in the morning, she mopped up his spilt drinks and she checked he'd washed his hands. She even transferred the peas off his plate onto her own without anyone noticing or before her brother could point out he never ate "stink-bombs".

Now, holding back thorny stems she helped the both the boys scramble through the overgrown jungle of hawthorn and elder trees down to their den. This secret hiding place was hacked out of the brambles of the disused railway line which ran along the bottom of their neighbouring gardens. The train track had been removed long ago and the area had become an overgrown tangle of bushes. It made the ideal place to discuss the crime; within shouting distance of home yet away from the interference of adults who weren't agile enough to tackle the steep slopes or avoid the vicious hawthorn spikes.

Older lads had tied ropes to the highest branches of the trees and although it meant suffering a lot of stings and scratches the more daring would swing from one side of the banks to the other. A few very brave youngsters egged on by their friends had even gone on expeditions into the dense woodland further down. Loaded catapults at the ready they would try to find the "giant turkey chickens" local legend said lived there.

Crawling through the opening into their camouflaged hideaway the three children were greeted, even on this warm day, by the comfortable smell of mushrooms and wet grass.

Lizzie sat down on a pile of moss and twisted a dark purple band tightly round her fingers before pulling her long, fair hair through it into a neat, tidy pony tail.

"For the last time Oliver," Lizzie told her brother. "The murderer isn't Slasher Smith. Slasher Smith doesn't really exist."

"He does!" Oliver corrected her.

"Who's this Slasher Smith?" Tom asked.

"Oh, for goodness sake Tom," Lizzie sighed. "Don't you start. Slasher Smith is a fictional character in one of Dad's old films. You know. The one about a man with hands made out of scissors. Oliver's watched it over and over again and now he thinks it's real." Turning to her younger brother she added, "Besides everybody knows he's not really scary."

"Well he may not be scary to Everybody but I wouldn't want to shake hands with a man who had knives instead of fingers!" Oliver replied.

"Oh you're hopeless," Lizzie laughed her blue eyes creasing into a smile.

"I bet it is Slasher Smith," Oliver continued.

"Shut up Oliver!" Tom said, running his fingers through his long dark hair. "You're talking nonsense as usual."

Lizzie got on well with Tom, they were the same age and could talk to each other easily, but her friend didn't have the patience she had with her younger brother. He did not always seem to understand or like some of the things Oliver said and did.

Propping himself up on his elbows Oliver ignored the others and pulled a couple of books out of the back pocket of his jeans. He flicked through a map book stopping now and then to sketch in a notepad.

With her brother occupied Lizzie carefully unfolded four newspaper clippings and laid them out on the dried grass that lined the floor of their den. Tom, his lanky legs tucked awkwardly under his tall skinny body, began to read,

"The Daily Mail's got,
GRIZZLY GOINGS ON IN ALLSWORTHY GRAVEYARD

The Mirror has,
ALLSWORTHY'S STREETS STAY SPOOKILY SILENT

The Sun can't find any,
SKELETONS IN ALLSWORTHY'S CUPBOARDS

And the Guardian says,
POLICE HAVE NO LEADS IN VILLAGE MURDER"

"The post mortem showed that the victim was in his late twenties." Lizzie was reading from one of the reports. "But British dental and finger print records show no matches."

"Is this what he looked like?" Tom asked pointing to a pencil drawing of a scrawny young man.

"Yes," Lizzie replied. "I wonder who he is."

"Mrs. Dale said he's probably a gipsy," Tom told his friend. "Although she said she hasn't seen any travellers in her shop for ages. They don't usually arrive until harvest time. Besides you'd still think someone would have reported him missing."

Without looking up from his sketching Oliver interrupted them. "P'raps he's an alien."

"Nope," Tom replied scanning the artist's impression of the man. "Nope, he's definitely not green and he doesn't appear to have any antennae."

Lizzie giggled but Oliver ignoring Tom explained. "P'raps he's an *illegal* alien."

"Oh, he means illegal immigrant," Lizzie said. "I suppose he could be from abroad. There have been all those people on the news trying to sneak into Britain."

"Then what on earth would he be doing in Allsworthy?" Tom said. "We're in the middle of the country, miles from the ports. No, he must be from round here somewhere.

"Who do you think killed him?" Lizzie asked.

"The police aren't saying much," Tom said after scouring the newspaper reports. "That means they don't have any clues." Tom liked to watch television detective shows and he was confident he knew how murder enquiries worked. "Mrs. Dale said she hasn't seen any strangers hanging around and she knows everyone so it must be somebody local."

"Ooh, d'you think we might know them? Personally I mean. Wouldn't it be great if we could find out who it was before the police?"

"Hmm, we need to work out a plan of action if we want to catch the killer," Tom said.

"Okay," Lizzie was already undoing the clasps on her rucksack. "I'll write down the things we're going to need, what we're going to do, and who we're going to interrogate."

Oliver continued to sketch as Lizzie started to make notes of all the local people they could interview to try and find some clues. P.C. Pane the village policeman was top of their list. Then Mrs. Dale the postmistress, old Harry the gravedigger, Mr. Jones and Mrs. Williams their schoolteachers...

She put down the questions they needed to ask and what they would be looking out for. "We'll have to follow up everything that seems suspicious no matter how small it might be," she said. "We'll need a camera, a tape recorder, a magnifying glass, notebooks, pencils..." Her list grew longer and longer. She forged on with her campaign like a general planning a battle while Tom read the newspaper articles and Oliver's pencil flew.

As Lizzie prattled on Tom glanced over at Oliver's drawing.

"What's he doing?" he asked surprised at what he saw.

"Oh, nothing," Lizzie replied without bothering to look up.

"I didn't know Oliver could draw." Tom said.

"He can't. He's completely hopeless at drawing. Just last week Miss Wells had a right go at me about her art lesson."

"Why?" Tom asked.

"Well apparently she'd spent the whole day arranging some roses for the class to draw. When she left the room for a minute Oliver stripped the leaves and petals off every stem till they were completely bare 'cos he thought they looked better that way."

"Sounds like something Oliver would do," Tom said.

"Yeah, but he caused such a kafuffle with the rest of the kids that when Miss Wells came back the Richardson twins were fighting a duel on a tabletop with two thorny stems, and little Emily Jackson was in floods of tears!"

"What did you say?" Tom asked.

"What could I say? Miss Wells shouldn't have left him they all know what he's like. Although… she is new. Actually I think it's her first teaching job. She was nearly in tears."

Then, lowering her voice so Oliver didn't overhear she whispered, "Anyway, the funny part is he thinks his picture's brilliant. He's so proud of it I put it up on the fridge door with a magnet, but it looks more like a stick insect than a flower!"

"Well," Tom insisted, "He's got some sort of talent. Look."

Oliver was busily scribbling away in his notebook drawing an exact copy of the street plan of Leicester city centre, marking every road, park, hospital and railway line, without once checking back to the map book.

"Look!" Tom said again. "This is wicked!"

"Yes." Lizzie glanced at her brother's artwork. "It's his party trick. Dad says he must have a photographic memory or something. But even though I've tried showing him how to do it he can't draw birds or people or anything real."

Chapter three.

Oh what a wondrous web we weave.

The next day the three friends took all the equipment they thought a detective would need and walked to the vicarage to interview Miss Mitchell the vicar.

"After all," Lizzie pointed out as they set off, "It makes sense to begin in the place it all started."

"How did you get the vicar to see us?" Tom wanted to know.

"I lied. I rang and told her we're making a village magazine and want to write an article about the murder. I said we're going to sell the magazine to raise money for the church roof so she couldn't refuse."

"Oh yeah," Tom agreed, "She's always raising money for something or another. My Dad refuses to go to anything she's going to be at."

Putting on his Dad's Somerset accent Tom said, "If t'ain't food collections for the starving nippers of 'Ollywood actors, it's vehicles t' transport three legged donkeys 'cross Outer Mongolia. I 'ave t'increase me overdraft at the bank every time I speak to 'er!"

Lizzie giggling at his impersonation said, "Do you remember when she did that calendar with the W.I. where they all took their clothes off and had their photos taken to raise money for the church?"

"Oh, yeah," Tom replied.

"And Miss Mitchell had her picture taken in the pulpit. She stood behind the lectern wearing only her dog collar!"

The boy shut his eyes and shuddered, "The calendar with all those old women in it was disgusting, wasn't it?"

"Yeah," Lizzie nodded. "But they raised enough money to put heating in the church and build the school a swimming pool."

"According to Dad the church officials wanted to chuck Miss Mitchell out." Tom told Lizzie. "But apparently they couldn't defrock her 'cos she hadn't been wearing a frock! That's my Dad's idea of a joke," he explained.

16

"Did you know she plays football for the Swan Inn?" Lizzie asked.

"Do I?" Tom replied. "Dad won't stop moaning about it. He gets really cheesed off 'cos she doesn't let the men have a chance to score any goals, she takes them all herself. Which I suppose considering she's thirty-something is pretty amazing!" After a short pause Tom added, "And she's got a wicked Harley-Davidson motorbike."

"She's not quite what you'd expect a lady vicar to be, is she?" Lizzie said.

✱

At ten o'clock exactly the three children stood in front of the wooden faces of cherubic angels who seemed to Lizzie to be smirking at them from the carved front door of the vicarage. The vast red brick building had such high windows that even if the dirty glass in the panes hadn't obscured their view the youngsters, even Tom who was the tallest of the three, could not have seen inside. Dying ivy, crinkled and brown, scrabbled at the crumbling brickwork and Lizzie felt such an unwelcome coldness ooze from the property that she lost her former self-assurance.

"Perhaps this isn't a good idea after all," she stammered.

Tom took no notice and pulled the iron handle of the vicarage doorbell firmly and for much longer than Lizzie would have dared. A metallic clanging drowned out the unexpected sound of a dog barking and after just a few moments wait Miss Mitchell opened the door and relaxed them with a warm smile.

"This is a wonderful idea of yours," she said. "I know the story you want to write about is a terrible tragedy but what could be a better idea than to turn it round so that some good can come out of it."

She ushered the children inside as she spoke and they found themselves in a huge entrance hall. A sudden cold draught swept down the wide oak staircase to greet them and all three children shivered in unison. Dirty footprints almost concealed the mosaic pattern of the tiled floor under their feet and Lizzie thought there was a funny smell like cooked cabbages hanging in the air.

Lizzie longed for a dog of her own so she looked round for the one they'd heard barking earlier but none came to meet them. She constantly pestered her mother to let her have a dog but Mrs. Pickles always said she had, "Enough on her plate trying to look after and feed Oliver."

Determined not to miss the chance to meet her favourite type of pet she asked, "Can we see your dog please?"

To her disappointment Miss Mitchell shook her head, "Don't have time for animals," she told Lizzie. "People are my priority. Now then," she went on, "The village could certainly do with cheering up after all the upheaval lately. I'm sure as well as this you'll find loads of other pleasanter news and fun things to write about in your magazine. Maybe you could put some puzzles in as well, eh?"

They followed her down a long gloomy passage pushing past piles of empty cardboard boxes until she stopped and opened a door with a round handle whose original shiny brass had over time turned a dull green gold. They stepped into a hazy misty room. Once their eyes grew used to the bright sunlight streaming in through the windows they could see it wasn't as Lizzie had first thought smoke from a fire that was clouding their view but dust swirling around in the sunbeams.

Lizzie gaped open mouthed at her surroundings. The dark wood panelling that covered the walls of the room appeared to be almost twice the height of the walls of their living room at home.

Row upon row of ancient leather bound dusty old books lined three of the walls. But it was the fourth wall that Lizzie stared at in horror. It was covered in dozens of gruesome trophies of deer, fox, wild boar and even buffalo heads. All stuffed and mounted on wooden plaques. As well as startled looking fish suspended inside glass cases. She glanced at the framed parchments of ancient maps and plans, yellowed and browning with age, which hung between the macabre collection. A couple of tatty, well-worn rugs were laid on the bare floorboards and dust and cobwebs covered every piece of furniture, every picture and every trophy.

"I thought we could talk in here," the vicar said. "I know these old chairs look a bit dilapidated but they're quite comfortable."

She pointed to a settee with horsehair sprouting out of holes in the grey upholstery and a chair which had great gashes slashed across the conker brown leather of its arms. The vicar plopped herself into a creaky wicker chair causing dust to puff out of the cushion and dangled her long legs carelessly over the sides like a rag doll hanging out of a toy box.

Lizzie trying not to look at the dead animals on the wall took a seat beside Tom on the settee and started to explain their mission in detail. Oliver, who didn't like to sit close to anyone, chose the armchair. He sat bolt upright, knees and ankles together, showing one charcoal grey and one black sock beneath trouser legs that were too short. He stared round the room taking in its contents as Lizzie asked, "Would you mind if we taped our conversation?"

Tom busily twiddling knobs and pushing levers was checking the recording levels on the tape recorder as she spoke. Looking up he said, "It'll make it easier when it comes to writing the article."

Miss Mitchell agreed so Lizzie started the interview.

The vicar had just told them about old Harry arriving puffing and wheezing and hammering on the vicarage door after finding the body when Oliver, who had not spoken yet, butted in. "It's very dirty in here."

"Oliver!" Lizzie said, her face turning red.

"Oh, he's quite right," Miss Mitchell laughed. "I'm afraid this old house is much too big for me to look after. In the old days the vicar would have been a married man and his poor wife and daughters would have spent all their time keeping on top of the housework. But I really don't do much at all. The Church Commissioners ought to sell it. I've told them a nice little cottage in the High Street would do me but they don't want to."

Once more Oliver interrupted, "There are more cobwebs in here than in Revenge of the Killer Spiders," he said.

This film had totally fascinated Oliver. He'd watched it over and over again collecting every spider he could find and storing them in jam jars on his bedroom windowsill. Lizzie could still remember the tantrum he'd thrown when their Mum had cleaned up his room and put them back in the wrong order.

"Except there!" Oliver exclaimed. "On that dead head." He pointed at a large stuffed stag's head on the far wall.

Lizzie realized that while they had been talking his blue eyes had been looking for anywhere the spiders had missed. And there on just one smooth and polished antler the spiders had run out of silk and been unable to finish their job of covering every part of the lifeless wildlife with cobwebs.

Oliver delighted with himself grinned in smug satisfaction as he sat back in his chair.

"I'm sorry," Lizzie started to apologize. "He doesn't mean to be rude he just says what he feels without thinking."

"He's fine," Miss Mitchell laughed again. "To be honest I wish I could take the hideous things down and burn them. I'm really only here as the Church custodian and I'm not supposed to alter anything without the say so of God himself."

She clasped her hands together, raised her eyes and pointed heavenward with one finger. A puzzled look crossed Oliver's face as he stared up towards the ceiling. He opened his mouth to speak but before he asked if he could go upstairs to see who was there, the vicar continued,

"Now, how about I get us some fruit juice and biscuits then perhaps Oliver will settle down so you can finish interviewing me."

Once the door of the room shut behind her Lizzie turned to Tom and asked if he had managed to get everything on tape.

"Well, there wasn't very much to record to be honest," he complained. "Most of it consists of Oliver spouting on about spiders and dead heads. Putting on a singsong voice he repeated Oliver word for word, *"There are more spiders in here than Revenge of the Killer Spiders"*.

"Oh don't tape things like that!" Lizzie exclaimed. "We'll never be able to make sense of it all if you tape that gibberish."

They sat waiting, a brooding silence hanging over them. A moment later their hostess came back into the room carrying a silver tray on which were four glasses full of juice and a pretty china plate piled high with biscuits.

"Now then, who wants something to eat?" she asked looking at Oliver who never refused food.

"I'd like a bacon sandwich," Oliver said.

Lizzie stepped in quickly. "There aren't any bacon sandwiches Oliver. There's orange juice and biscuits. Oh and look they're your favourites," she added noticing the chocolate chip cookies.

"I don't want biscuits. I want a bacon sandwich. Like you!" he said. He stared hard at the vicar as if daring her to deny that she hadn't got one hidden somewhere.

At that moment both Lizzie and Tom realized that they could also detect a faint but definite whiff of bacon cooking although the delicious smell seemed to be coming up from below them from underneath the floorboards!

The vicar too could obviously smell it now for she immediately started to sniff the air curiously. Then her expression changed. She frowned slightly. She stiffened and it seemed to Lizzie she had grown at least two inches taller.

She paused then said, "Oh that'll be old Harry cooking himself a mid morning snack. He uses my kitchen now he's on his own. I think he likes the company and the free food."

Oliver was not to be put off. "I really would like a bacon sandwich. I only had one bowl of cereals for breakfast this morning because she," Oliver pointed an accusing finger at his sister, "Said I didn't have time for toast!"

The vicar's mood changed and her mouth set straight and taut like an overloaded fishing line before it snaps. "Well," she said sharply. "I can see that your brother has set his heart on a bacon sandwich so you'd better take him home and cook him one Lizzie."

Lizzie blushed even more. Realizing they had now overstayed their welcome she and Tom packed up their gear offering their thanks and apologies to the vicar all at the same time.

Lizzie and Tom shooed Oliver out of the vicarage in silence. Once outside though Lizzie tried to tell her brother off. She explained the right and wrong ways to behave in company saying, "It's very rude to interrupt people when they're talking." But Lizzie knew Oliver wasn't listening. He was too busy humming a tune to himself.

Chapter four.

Ironing out problems.

Lizzie and Tom argued, nagged and blamed each other like an old married couple all the way home.

Tom moaned, "It'll be impossible to detect anything all the time Oliver keeps interfering."

Lizzie shouted at her friend. "You know that when Mum and Dad are at work I have to look after him. He can't be left alone he wouldn't know what to do in an emergency."

"*What* emergency?" Tom shouted back. "What could *possibly* happen?"

"Well, there *is* a killer on the loose!" Lizzie said.

"*Oh there is a killer on the loose,*" Tom mocked.

Oliver ignored them both and once home he took himself off to watch a film in his bedroom. He went up the stairs with a bacon sandwich clutched in one hand and, with the thought of cobwebs fresh on his mind, Revenge of the Killer Spiders in the other.

Tom slouched in an armchair channel hopping from one TV programme to another. Lizzie, moving a shopping survey her mum was filling in put a bacon sandwich on the coffee table in front of him.

"That's it!" she suddenly exclaimed. "We'll write out forms and give them to everyone to complete. Then when we collect them in we'll cross check everything to see if anyone's lying."

"Brilliant!" Tom cried sitting up straight. "That should speed up the process too and hopefully stop Oliver asking Mrs. Dale if she's so fat because she eats all the sweets in her shop."

"Yes," Lizzie laughed her spirits lifting. "Or telling P.C. Pane our TV licence expired last week."

"Did it?" asked Tom quickly switching off the set.

"No not really Stupid," Lizzie giggled. "But don't switch it back on we have to decide what to ask people."

Working as a team again they spent the afternoon picking the best questions to find who had no alibi or who seemed suspicious.

Questions such as:

- Where were you at the time the murder took place?
- Who were you with?
- Where were you when you heard about the murder?
- Who were you with then?
- What did you say when you heard about the murder?
- What did your companion say?

"Anyone who objects to filling in the form must have something to hide so they can go straight to the top of our suspect list," said Lizzie.

"Who exactly is on our suspect list at the moment?" asked Tom.

"Well no one as yet," Lizzie said. "But if Oliver doesn't watch himself I might be the prime suspect for murdering him!"

*

They decided for safety they would only deliver forms to people they knew but as they knew most of the village it still meant a lot of work. Despite Tom's hope this would be quicker than interviewing people it still took hours walking up and down the village streets, unlatching and latching garden gates, posting the papers through endless letterboxes.

"I *never* want to be a postman," said Tom. "This is taking for ever."

"It'd be quicker if you jumped the gates," Oliver suggested. "Then you wouldn't waste so much time opening and shutting them again."

He refused to go up to most people's doors after a barking dog frightened him but this didn't stop him from giving advice.

"*It'd be quicker if you jumped the gates!*" Tom sang. "Go on then Clever Clogs," he dared. "Show us how to do it."

24

Before Lizzie could stop him Oliver took a long stumbling run, his arms flailing wildly, up to the low looped chain which circled a neighbour's front lawn.

Had the chain had been six inches lower or had Oliver jumped six inches higher everything would have been fine. Unfortunately he caught his foot in the white plastic links and with a dive that any swimming teacher would have been proud of landed face down in the middle of a bed of petunias. The flowers lay flattened beneath him as the entire length of chain fencing trailed behind his left foot.

It took over a quarter of an hour for Tom and Lizzie to replace the fence while Oliver attempted to revive each and every squashed petunia.

Several villagers stopped to chat about what they were doing. Oliver's explanation that they were, "Making a magazine to catch a killer and mend the church roof," left most of them a little baffled. But the children's project amused most of them and nearly all of them agreed to take part.

The only person who objected to filling in their form was Mrs. Dale the short tempered and quick-tongued postmistress.

"I'm up at four o'clock each morning as it is. I don't have time for this nonsense," she grumbled.

But her husband took the sheet of paper from the children and told them to collect it later which saved her from going to the top of the suspect list.

When they went back for it his wife was in a better mood.

"So which one of you is Sherlock Holmes and which Dr Watson?" she asked. Both her chins wobbled furiously as she chuckled to herself.

Oliver opened his mouth to speak but Lizzie remembering Tom's earlier concerns quickly shoved her brother out of the shop before he could make any rude comments about the shopkeeper's weight. Once outside Oliver was very cross.

"Why wasn't I allowed to ask Mrs. Dale if she'd seen the 1939 Sherlock Holmes film the Hound of the Baskervilles starring Basil Rathbone. I wanted to know what she thought of it. I think it's the best version ever made."

✦

Three days later and before they'd got round to contacting him P.C. Pane the village policeman visited the children. They knew the large, jovial man well because he gave road safety talks at the school. He also ran cycling proficiency lessons where he used to show off his own skill and maturity by "bunny hopping" and doing "wheelies" to the delighted squeals of his easily impressed audience.

P.C. Pane recognized Oliver immediately. "Oliver me lad, did you watch that documentary last night about the great white shark? Good stuff, eh?"

Oliver spent his time during the cycling lessons running alongside the officer talking about their shared passion for dolphins, sharks and other sea creatures. He didn't have the coordination to ride a bike himself but he liked to be included in the sessions and he enjoyed sharing his interest with the policeman who listened to his lectures on marine life. Unfortunately Oliver's style of running, like a drunken windmill lurching from side to side, made him a hazard for the other children. Cycling in and out of cones they found it impossible to avoid both their classmate and the stationary obstacles. So very often the young cyclists returned home with grazed knees and bruised pride.

Now as the officer waited for Lizzie to fetch a form to show him he glanced around the Pickles' cosy living room taking in the comfortable but shabby furniture and the stack of videos piled up in front of the television set. He noticed a half completed jigsaw puzzle laid out on the dining room table and went over to take a closer look.

"Don't do that!" Lizzie cried as she walked back into the room carrying a pile of papers and a slice of cream cake for each of them. The officer's head jerked up and he looked at her in surprise his hand hovering over the spot where he felt sure the piece of puzzle he held would fit in.

"I'm sorry," Lizzie apologized to the helpful policeman. "Dad doesn't like anyone fiddling with his jigsaws, even Mum isn't allowed to touch them."

"Aw," P.C. Pane said disappointed at not being allowed to contribute to the puzzle. "Then what do you do when it's dinner time?" he asked, seeing all the jigsaw pieces scattered across the table.

"We sit here on the settees," the girl replied. "We eat off trays."

"No we don't!" Oliver corrected her in astonishment. "We eat off plates!"

P.C. Pane laughed and plopped himself down next to the boy not noticing Oliver's piece of cake that had been left on the seat.

"No!" Oliver cried as the officer lurched back up to his feet. But too late, the Black Forest gateau and the plate were glued to his large backside.

While Mrs. Pickles washed his cream, cherry and chocolate stained trousers the policeman, unable to fit into her husband's clothes, sat with a towel wrapped round him and looked at the children's form.

"I'm rather concerned about you getting involved in a police enquiry," he explained in his slow, gentle Midlands accent. "I 'm not sure that I should let you carry on with this really. You 'ave to very careful what you ask people these days," he said.

He tried to dissuade them from continuing, "You can never be too sure what will come from asking folks questions sometimes they give you answers you don't expect."

Oliver looked at the officer in surprise. "If you knew what the answers were going to be you wouldn't need to ask questions," he started to explain to the policeman.

Tom quickly interrupted him. "Shut up Oliver. Listen, I think your Mum wants you in the kitchen. He's just coming Mrs. Pickles," he shouted to Oliver's mum as he shooed his friend out of his own living room.

Tom sat down beside the officer saying, "It's all just harmless fun and it's for a good cause. It'll be invaluable experience for me too 'cos I want to join the police force when I finish school."

In the kitchen once the quick wash cycle had finished the children's mother began to carefully iron dry the policeman's trousers. Oliver looked on growing more and more frustrated as she failed to remove the thick long crease running the length of each leg.

When Mrs. Pickles went to answer the telephone ringing in the hallway Oliver, no longer able to put up with her slapdash work, took over from her. Mrs. Pickles returned to the smell of burning cloth and the sight of Oliver trying to separate P.C. Pane's trousers from a steaming hot iron.

Before he set off to cycle home Lizzie handed the police officer a form to fill in. He took it saying, "Remember don't give these to anyone you don't know. I'll return mine later on. I'll bring it round with a video about dolphins I've got for young Oliver." Then as he rode away on his bicycle his regulation navy blue jacket lifted to show a pair of Union Jack underpants peeping through a hole in his uniform trousers.

Chapter five.

Things start to heat up.

The following day Lizzie received a phone call from their neighbour Doreen. The youngsters often used to go and chat to the retired farmer's wife as she would feed them all sorts of home-made cakes and treats. Oliver enjoyed visiting her. He would stay for hours relating scene by scene the latest film he'd watched. Or he'd explain in minute detail the life cycle of a great white shark at the same time tucking into a huge plateful of jam and cream scones.

Doreen was calling from a mobile phone as she travelled along the motorway but interference made the call difficult to hear.

"Can you go round and feed the cats," Lizzie thought she said. "And water the plants in the greenhouse. We're going to Scotland to look after our daughter and brand new grandson for a few days. I'm sorry it's short notice. The baby's come early and I was in such a dither this morning I forgot all about the cats."

Lizzie could hear Doreen only faintly down the crackly line but after reassuring her that they knew where she kept everything and what to do she hung up and went in search of Oliver.

He didn't like cats very much. As he explained to Lizzie, "I don't trust cats. Their claws are sharp and so are their teeth. And you can never tell how they're going to react. Sometimes they purr when you stroke them but sometimes they lash out and hiss and scratch for no reason. No I don't trust cats," he finished. But he would do anything to please Doreen and strangely her three pets Molly, Polly and Dolly seemed to like him and always made a beeline for him whereas they usually hid from Lizzie.

The brother and sister called round for Tom on their way but Tom's mum told Lizzie that he and his dad were taking advantage of the lovely sunny day and they'd gone fishing and she didn't know when to expect them back. So they went round to Doreen's house without him.

Lizzie let them in with the spare key she found under the pot of mint by the back door and set about looking for the cat food, tin opener and bowls. It didn't take her very long to find everything she needed in the clean, tidy little kitchen. Meanwhile Oliver went into the back garden to call the cats but returned after just a couple of minutes saying, "We can go home. The cats don't need feeding. They're not here."

"Of course they're here!" Lizzie told him. "They're just hiding that's all. Come on we'll go and look for them together."

But although they called, "Molly, Polly, Dolly," over and over again Oliver was absolutely right. There was no sign of them.

Doreen and her husband loved growing plants and the garden consisted of many different areas to explore. Their green fingers had created a well-stocked vegetable patch as well as beautiful flowerbeds and even a small pear and apple orchard at the far end. After his visits Oliver used to go home laden with carrier bags full of cooking apples or lettuces and tomatoes.

The sun beat down on Lizzie and Oliver as they searched all through the long garden; checking the empty coal bunker, looking under every bush and behind every Brussels sprout plant. But they could not find the elusive animals.

They looked up in the branches of the fruit trees to see if they had got stuck up there. No luck.

"It's no good," said Lizzie. "We'll just have to leave the food in the greenhouse and hope that the cats come for it when they get hungry. We'll check all the nooks and crannies in case they've got themselves stuck somewhere."

She fetched the key for the padlock and let them both in. The greenhouse went a long way back and watering Doreen's wilting tomatoes as they went they pushed past exotic flora like explorers in the Amazon rain forest.

They peered into every possible spot a cat could hide in with Oliver even checking under upturned flowerpots. Eventually having no success they turned round and retraced their footsteps.

They found the door shut fast when they reached it although Lizzie thought she had just pulled it to. It wouldn't budge when she tried to open it and then she noticed why. The shiny silver padlock had shut back down on itself and the large well-oiled bolt on the door would not open no matter how hard she tried to shake it free.

Oliver began to fidget in the stuffy air of the hot greenhouse. Lizzie could feel him standing so close that his warm breath dampened the hair on the back of her head.

He started hopping from foot to foot, "Will we get out in time for lunch? I'm hungry. I want to go home now. Mum will have lunch ready soon. We mustn't be late."

Lizzie needed her brother to be quiet so she could think clearly. "Sit down here," she told him pointing to an old plank of wood that wobbled on top of some loose bricks. "I can see the key in the padlock I've just got to work out how to reach it," she explained in as calm a voice as possible.

At first she thought that she would simply have to break a pane of glass. When she looked closer at the windows she realized they weren't glass at all but were made out of thick tough plastic. She picked up an old wooden handled trowel she found lying in a corner and bashed hard against a section of the door. As she suspected it had no effect at all, it simply jarred against her hand and after several more attempts the handle fell off the trowel.

By now Oliver was becoming very agitated at the thought of missing his lunch, babbling away and bobbing up and down on the makeshift bench that Lizzie had sat him on.

"It's hot in here, isn't it?" he asked his sister. "I'm ever so hot, ever so hot," he repeated again and again.

Lizzie knew she needed to calm him. "Looks as if we're just going to have to wait until Mum and Dad come for us," she said, as confidently as she could manage. But she wasn't sure how long that would be and she didn't know if she would be able to keep Oliver relaxed and occupied for much longer; not without food or drink to keep him quiet. Her own throat felt dry, probably from fear she realized. She knew that in the ever-increasing heat they would soon start to get very thirsty indeed.

Perspiration trickled down her forehead but it wasn't just the air in the greenhouse that was making her sweat. She wondered how soon it would be before they were missed and how long could they survive in the hothouse without anything to drink.

Suddenly they heard the sound of footsteps running down the garden path and a familiar voice called out their names. Relief flooded over Lizzie as Tom's nose pressed against the misted window and peered in at them.

It took just a couple of seconds for him to turn the key in the lock and release them from their prison. When he had Tom explained that on returning home to fetch some forgotten bait he'd heard about Lizzie's visit.

"I knew something was wrong straight away 'cos I saw Doreen in the shop earlier in the week and she told me they were leaving for a holiday to Spain on Thursday. She'd arranged for the cats to go into a cattery and a gardener to see to the plants. Her daughter's baby isn't due for at least three months!"

Lizzie felt sick as the thought they could have been shut in the greenhouse for a long time hit her.

"Don't be daft," Tom laughed. "People would soon have started looking for you when you didn't turn up for dinner. Everybody knows Oliver wouldn't be late for a meal. Still," he added, "Makes you wonder who phoned you this morning and how the greenhouse door managed to shut and lock itself behind you doesn't it? Looks as if someone's trying to stop us." Grinning he added, "Which means we must be getting warmer!"

Chapter six.

The butcher of Allsworthy.

Once back home Lizzie wanted to phone P.C. Pane straightaway. Tom stopped her saying, "No don't call him. Whoever trapped you in Doreen's greenhouse must be worried we're on to something. They wanted to scare you so we'd give up. We don't want the police interfering just as things are looking interesting."

"I don't know," Lizzie said. "Anything could have happened if you'd not come along when you did."

But Tom persisted, "You know P.C. Pane wasn't very keen about us doing this in the first place. *I'm not sure I should let you carry on really,*" he mimicked the policeman. "If he finds out about this he definitely won't let us continue. Look we've already had six questionnaires returned and there are lots more due back soon. Let's go over what we've got so far and see if we can spot any clues."

They read each one through to see if anyone had written anything out of the ordinary. But despite reading them several times they couldn't find anything that suggested foul play.

The only person who seemed at all suspicious was Jim Harper the local butcher.

"He's really strong," said Lizzie.

"Yeah I know," Tom replied. "I've seen him sling a whole pig's carcass over his shoulder then hang it on a hook at the back of his shop like he's hanging out washing. My mum says he's really fit," Tom continued. "He trains for the football team by jogging round the village before anyone else is up. She says he looks cute in his shorts and T shirt, especially when it's pouring with rain."

"What's your mum doing up watching him?" Lizzie asked.

"I dunno. But she says he's very agile for his age."

An accident at a pheasant shoot one autumn had left the butcher blinded in an eye and his cold unblinking stare disturbed Lizzie.

"I didn't used to know where to look," she told Tom. "I felt really uncomfortable answering him when he spoke to me. I didn't know which eye to look at. Not till Mum said I should look him straight between the eyebrows, it was alright after that."

When they thought about it both Lizzie and Tom realized their memories of the man were not pretty. They had watched him sharpen knives on the hard steel block at the back of his counter, seen him wipe his hands on a blood stained apron or waited as he cut slices of ham on a huge, electric machine that whirred dangerously close to his fingers.

"Mum's told me there's a special guard on the cutter to protect his hands but I always hold my breath until he's finished just in case something goes wrong," Lizzie admitted.

Now to add to their concerns the butcher had written in the comment's box on his form,

"If you have any idea when the police will be finished with the shears could you ask they be returned to me as I could do with them for shearing some sheep."

"I suppose he thinks he's being funny," said Tom. "Well just wait till he wakes up murdered one morning. He won't be laughing then!"

Lizzie sat deep in thought. Then as a dreadful idea struck her she cried out, "Supposing Jim Harper's been murdering people and making meat pies and sausages out of their bodies!"

The idea made her tummy heave but Tom didn't seem to have such a sensitive stomach. "Hmm. It would explain why his sausages are so tasty," he replied.

"Yeah that's right," Lizzie quickly got over her feelings of sickness. "They're made to a secret recipe that's been handed down through the Harper family. Mum always says once you've tried their sausages you can never go back to any others."

They decided they would keep a very close eye on Jim Harper the butcher and Lizzie already had an idea how they could do just that.

*

Later that day old Harry turned up at Lizzie's house.

"Sorry it's taken so long." The inky blue veins showed up like a tattoo on the back of his hand as he held out his form.

"Left school at thir'een and not had much use for read'n 'n wri'ing since then. It takes me a while to get me 'ead round it all."

Mrs. Pickles invited him in for a cup of tea. As the old man hobbled over their doorstep he took off his cap and moaned, "This darn heat's getting to me."

Once inside their cosy kitchen he laid down his cap and walking stick and settled into a chair happy to have someone to talk to. The murder had made him quite famous in the village but now that the press had gone things were returning to their usual routine and he missed all the attention. He took his mug of tea and stirred in five spoonfuls of sugar. When he noticed the children staring at him open mouthed he grinned toothlessly,

"Aar I likes me sugar it gives me th'energy to dig all them graves." He held the mug of tea with one hand and with the other grabbed a fistful of biscuits out of a tin. These he proceeded to dunk one after the other into his cup.

Oliver who had been watching all this in silence could not keep quiet any longer. "I want a cup of tea Mum," he demanded forgetting to say please.

Lizzie thought it odd as Oliver did not like tea. Now her brother copied the old man's actions and helped himself to a pile of biscuits which he also dunked in his drink. Unfortunately he left the biscuits in the tea for too long so that as he lifted them out each one fell back into his mug with a splosh.

Lizzie could see her mother was getting cross so she said, "Harry, tell us how you found the body."

Just as he was describing the look on the vicar's face Mr. Pickles the children's father burst into the kitchen and started sorting through the clutter on top of the dresser. He did not notice their visitor until his wife pointed him out. Mr. Pickles nodded at Harry then asked if anyone knew where the missing piece was.

"Piece of what?" asked Mrs. Pickles.

"The jigsaw!" her husband shouted. "There's a piece missing. Has anyone moved it?"

Everyone, including old Harry, shook their heads in reply but by this time Mr. Pickles had given up searching the dresser and was now running upstairs to look there.

Shrugging her shoulders Mrs. Pickles went over to the sink and began peeling potatoes. Remembering their guest she asked, "Would you like to stay for dinner Harry?"

They all knew that since his wife had died a couple of years ago the old man lived alone. Lizzie guessed her mum thought he could probably do with some good old fashioned home cooking.

"It's only bangers and mash I'm afraid but you're very welcome to share it with us and they're Harper's sausages of course."

Lizzie and Tom looked at each other as they remembered their talk about what the sausages might have in them.

But Harry screwed up his nose and said, "That's very kind of you me duck but if you don't mind I'd rather get back to me cheese 'n pickle cobs I got wait'n for me at home. Since I buried that young Lacey girl last year I've not been able t' touch meat." Shaking his head he added, "She died o' that ESP you know."

Oliver stopped fishing around for the soggy remains of the dunked biscuits and looked up in surprise.

"Extra Sensory Perception!" he said. "I didn't know you could die from that!"

"I think Harry means BSE," Tom explained politely. "It's Bovine Encepha something or another. Mad cow disease to you and me."

Tom seemed determined not to let Harry leave without finding out everything he knew about the murder. "Who do you suspect Harry? Didn't you notice anything unusual that day? Any cars parked in the car park you didn't recognize?"

But Harry didn't have anything to add. He gave one of two replies to everything he was asked, either "I couldn'a say really," or "I really dunno".

At last realizing he was unable to help them solve the mystery of the murder Harry scratched the top of his head.

"It's dead puzzlin' ain't it?" he said.

Oliver looked closely at a biscuit before lowering it to its watery grave. "It's not the dead who are puzzling," he said. "It's the living."

They all turned to stare at him as they tried to work out what he was going on about but Oliver was busy watching the remains of a sodden digestive slip from his teaspoon into the dregs at the bottom of his cup.

The resultant splash showered a large brown tea stain all over the snow-white tablecloth.

Harry took this as his cue to leave and pulling his cap firmly on to his bald head and bidding a "goodnight to y'all," the old man ambled stiffly off into the darkening twilight in search of his supper.

Chapter seven.

Oliver does a vanishing trick.

Lizzie and Tom decided that the next day they would take a picnic to the park so they could keep watch on the butcher in case their gruesome suspicions about the meat in his "Home-Made Produce" were correct.

"Mum said Sunday is the day he gets his sausages and pies made up ready to sell Monday morning," Lizzie told Tom. "If we get there early enough and sit by the bandstand we should be able to watch Jim Harper as he's coming and going. I don't know if we'll be able to see inside the butcher's but we should spot any deliveries that are made round the back."

"What about You Know Who?" her friend asked under his breath glancing in Oliver's direction.

"You don't have to come if you don't want to Oliver." Lizzie tried suggesting. "It will be ever so boring just sitting there with nothing to do all day."

But Oliver was not to be put off and he busied himself packing a rucksack with everything they would need for the day: binoculars, tape recorder, his A to Z, notebook, pencils, crisps...

"Have we no crisps?" he asked on finding there was only one pack to share between the three of them.

"We don't need crisps we'll make some sandwiches and there are plenty of apples in the fruit bowl we'll take them with us." Lizzie said.

"We must have crisps," Oliver insisted. "You can't have a picnic without crisps!"

In the end to stop his nagging his sister agreed that he could go to the shop first thing in the morning to buy some.

Lizzie should have known it was not going to be a good day when the next morning she was woken at five a.m. by the sound of the telephone ringing and her parents, shouting.

Mrs. Dale had phoned to say that Oliver was on her doorstep demanding to be let in so he could buy some crisps.

"It's not right!" Lizzie, sitting in her pyjamas beside her weary mum on the bottom stair, could hear the postmistress screeching down the telephone. "People shouldn't have to put up with this! Can't you keep control of your children? Don't you realize what long hours we work? I rarely get more than six hours sleep at the best of times. I'm up at six o'clock every day as it is."

Mr. Pickles was hauled out of bed and sent to collect his confused and angry son from the store. Once home Oliver argued that if the sun was up it must be first thing and Lizzie had promised that he could go to the shop first thing.

"Besides," he told his family, "Everyone heard Mrs. Dale say she got up at four o'clock each morning so she must be a liar because she wasn't today!"

With the threat of being grounded for not just that day but the entire summer holiday Lizzie did her best to persuade her mum and dad to let them carry on with the picnic. She told her parents they could get some rest while she and Tom looked after Oliver for the whole day. She kept their spying mission on the butcher to herself and eventually her mum sighed and said that they could go so long as she took Oliver back to the shop to apologize.

At eight o'clock when Mrs. Dale opened the store Lizzie and Oliver were the first customers on her doorstep. Oliver still wasn't sure that he should say he was sorry but after Lizzie offered to buy several bags of various flavoured crisps he agreed.

By eight thirty with the sun promising a scorching hot day the three children had positioned themselves in the park so they had a clear view of the back of the row of shops, including the butchers. They settled down on the grass in the hope they would find a clue that would help them solve the mystery.

Time ticked by slowly but nothing out of the ordinary happened. Jim Harper only lived across the park from his butcher's shop but they did not see him walking to work as they had hoped. The bars that had been fitted to the back windows of all the shops following a break in earlier in the year made it impossible to see anything that was going on inside.

They watched as the congregation made its way to church for the morning service and they watched it leave at the end. As the sun rose higher in the sky it got hotter and hotter and with no breeze to cool them down the trio had to move to the shade of some horse chestnut trees.

They ate their picnic earlier than planned as Oliver couldn't wait until twelve o'clock and they squabbled over which crisps they wanted.

"Sorry Oliver," Tom teased. "The cheese and onion ones have all gone there's only salt and vinegar left."

"Oh no they haven't!" Oliver had kept a careful check on his favourites. "There's a packet behind you!"

The only time anything interesting happened was when they saw Mrs. Dale make several trips out of the back of the Post Office just before it closed at midday. At the distance they were the children could not tell what was in the carrier bags she held but they did see her empty something into one of the bins that stood in the car park next to the children's playground.

"Maybe she's in league with Jim Harper," Lizzie suggested. "Perhaps that was bits of the bodies they can't get rid of!"

"Gimme a break," Tom said. "I don't think a butcher would have a problem getting rid of body parts."

"Why wouldn't he?" Lizzie asked.

Tom sighed. "Well to start with he must know a pig farmer and pigs will eat anything and everything. Or anyone! Besides even if they couldn't get rid of the bodies I'm sure they'd find somewhere better than the paper recycling bin!"

Disgusted at the vivid images flashing through her mind of a pig picnicking on human remains and annoyed at Tom's rebuke Lizzie turned her back on him. Although it was very difficult on such a lovely summer's day she tried to sulk. But the scent of newly mown grass and a blackbird's cheerful song high up in the branches above their heads meant that her bad mood soon passed.

She forgot about Tom's remarks and watched bees buzzing lazily past her zig zagging from clover to clover. Suddenly the peace was shattered when one bee got too close for Oliver's comfort making him roar in panic. He leapt to his feet and raced round the park shrieking loudly. Waving his arms in the air above his head he swatted at the bee that had long since lost interest in him and was now nowhere near.

Tom shouted at Oliver to be quiet but the boy carried on screaming. Lizzie jumped up and chased after him trying to make him realize that the bee had gone and he was safe.

Only the offer of the last packet of smoky bacon crisps calmed him and at last he settled down with these, the notebook and pencils and started to doodle.

"I do wish Oliver wasn't quite so much hard work sometimes," she said to Tom as she threw herself on the grass beside him.

Once again Tom managed to upset her by saying, "My twin cousins are just like Oliver they'd have done exactly the same thing."

"But they're only three it's not quite the same is it?" She felt sad that even though he was her best friend he didn't understand.

This, together with her early morning start and the sweltering heat, increased Lizzie's grumpiness. She felt tired and her head ached and she could not be bothered to talk to either of the two boys at this moment. Her eyelids became heavier and heavier and she shut them while she listened to the birdsong. "That pigeon sounds odd," Lizzie mumbled as she caught the sound of a distant, "coo coo".

"That's because it's a cuckoo." Tom replied. He began to recite,

"In April, come he will,
In May, sing all day,
In June, changes tune,
In July, prepare to fly,
In August, go he must."

But Lizzie didn't hear the last line as she was already fast asleep so Tom stopped and shut his eyes too. Only Oliver continued scribbling away on the sheets of blank white paper in front of him.

The birds had stopped singing when Lizzie woke up and it was very hot. Despite her nap she still felt groggy and uncomfortable. Her head was throbbing as if strapped up with an elastic band and her bad mood had returned. She looked round for the two boys but although Tom was snoozing peacefully beside her Oliver was nowhere to be seen.

Lizzie shook Tom awake. "Where's Oliver gone?" She shouted.

"I don't know," Tom yawned and stretched his arms. "He was here just a minute ago."

They ran round the park looking for him everywhere but Oliver had disappeared.

Chapter eight.

Oliver's made plans.

The day was now so hot and the air so heavy that as Lizzie and Tom ran round the park their legs dragged like they were running through deep water. They stopped, puffing and panting.

"He can't be far away," gasped Tom. "He was right here drawing. Perhaps he's left a note."

They looked at the notepad but there was no message, just page after page of scribbled drawings covering every square inch of paper. The sketches puzzled the children.

"What's this?" Tom asked. He rubbed his bleary eyes to help him focus.

"I'm not sure," Lizzie replied as she peered at the sheet.

"It looks like a sort of house plan," Tom continued. "Like an architect would draw only different. And what do these words say?"

Lizzie snatched the paper out of Tom's hands and looked at it closely as she tried to make out her brother's scrawled spidery handwriting.

"It's the vicarage," she said at last. "He's drawn a plan of the vicarage showing all the different floors and everything. Where on earth has he got this idea from?"

"Don't you remember?" Tom asked after a moment's pause. "When we talked to the vicar Oliver sat staring at those maps and things on the walls. I bet this was among them. You said he had a photographic memory."

"I wonder if he's gone there," Lizzie said. "Do you think he's gone to the vicarage?"

"What on earth for?" replied Tom.

Lizzie couldn't think straight she felt as if her brain were melting in the heat of the sun but she knew she had to try to find her brother.

"I don't know," she cried. "But we can't just sit here doing nothing. Come on the vicar should be at home by now getting ready for tonight's service. Let's go and see if Oliver's there."

✱

"I'm sorry." Miss Mitchell scowled down at them as Lizzie asked about Oliver. She seemed quite aloof today and her voice was sharp. "I haven't seen your brother since you all came round the other day."

Then seeing Lizzie's concern she continued, "I shouldn't worry I doubt if any harm has come to him. Why don't you scout round the village and see if he's invited himself into dinner somewhere. Better hurry up though," she added glancing up at the sky. "Looks as if a storm's brewing."

She seemed to be in a hurry to get rid of the two friends and almost shut the door in their faces. They turned round and made their way back up the long driveway. As they walked past a bush Tom stopped, stared for a second then darted underneath and scrabbled around in the soil below the large, shiny leaves. He came out waving a book in the air.

"Look!" He shouted. "Look!"

It was Oliver's A to Z map book.

"He had that with him this morning," Lizzie said. "What's it doing here on the vicarage driveway?"

"And without Oliver!" Tom was onto the clue like an excited bloodhound. "*And* with the vicar saying that Oliver hadn't been here! Somebody's telling us porky pies!" Tom glanced back at the big house as he spoke.

"Porky what?" asked Lizzie.

"Porky pies.... lies!" Tom translated. "Miss Mitchell's lying to us. Oliver's been here."

"Pork pies..." Lizzie stood thinking. "Yes, there's something else that's been bothering me about her...." she stopped mid sentence.

"What?" Tom asked.

46

"I don't know for sure," Lizzie continued. "But I think it's got something to do with pork..... Oh I don't know. I just have this feeling I don't trust her but I don't know why."

Lizzie shivered even though the sun was beating down on them. "I don't like this Tom!" She stared at the map book that Tom was still holding trying to decide what to do. "I think we'd better call the police."

"And tell them what?" Tom asked. "That a nine year old boy's been missing for half an hour! They won't take any notice of us they'll just laugh. You have to have been gone for ages before they start looking for you. And if we tell them we think he's been kidnapped by the vicar they'll think we're mad and lock *us* up. Then we'll never find him. No," Tom shook his head. "We've got to have more than a map book to go on. We need proof."

"I don't care if they think we're mad or not!" Lizzie cried. "Oliver's not like other nine year old boys. He's.... well he needs.... looking out for more," she finished.

What could she say to Tom? For the second time that day she thought her best friend ought to understand how worried she was about her little brother.

"We've got to do something," Lizzie shouted. "Think Tom! Think!"

"I think you should calm down." Tom said. "I also think real detectives would go back to headquarters, look at everything they've got and try to make sense of it all. We ought to tell your Mum and Dad what's happened too," he added.

"No. It'll worry them to death," said Lizzie. "We've got to find Oliver before anything happens to him. I daren't go back without him."

Chapter nine.

Oliver's not so clueless.

When Lizzie and Tom entered "headquarters" or Tom's house as it was usually called his dad was just carving an enormous leg of roast lamb.

"I might'a guessed you two'd turn up. Now there won't be enough for us," he joked. "Phew! That's a relief! Oliver's not with you. He always eats us out of house and home!"

Lizzie had no appetite but Mrs. White insisted. "Come on there's plenty for everyone. Sit yourself down here dear."

Lizzie loved Mrs. White's cooking but today she found it impossible to eat. Even the Yorkshire pudding oozing with mint sauce and tasty gravy stuck in her throat. She pushed slices of carrot and chunks of crispy roast potatoes round her plate until eventually Rusty, Tom's old black and white spaniel, came to her rescue by lying at her feet and wolfing down the food she passed to him.

When the dessert turned out to be rice pudding Lizzie politely refused saying, "Thanks, really Mrs. White, but I'm so full I couldn't eat another thing."

Tom's mum however wasn't going to take no for an answer, "You don't have to worry about putting on weight dear you're too slim as it is."

Luckily Tom's Dad saved her by scooping Lizzie's bowlful of pudding into his own and giving her a wink said, "Some Chinese farmer's worked 'is socks off to produce this rice. If you think I'm gonna let that dog 'ave it you've got another blinking thought coming!"

Tom had to gulp the creamy dessert down in great mouthfuls while Lizzie kept nudging him in the ribs to hurry up. At last they escaped to his bedroom where Tom set up his dart's scoreboard to act as their chart and they listed everything they thought important.

After a time Lizzie put her ear to the recorder and said, "Listen, can you hear music playing?"

Tom turned up the volume but he couldn't hear what Lizzie's sharp ears could. At last with the recorder playing at full volume he could just pick up a slow, sad, haunting tune.

"I wonder why we didn't hear it when we were at the vicarage," Lizzie asked.

"I expect we were too busy apologizing for Oliver," Tom answered.

"You know I think that's the tune he was humming when we came away," Lizzie said as they listened to it again. "He doesn't miss as much as we think he does," she said. "I wonder where it's coming from."

"Perhaps Harry was playing the violin at the same time as he was cooking his bacon sandwiches," Tom joked.

Lizzie gasped. "That's it!" she cried.

Tom stared at her open mouthed. "What? Harry's a musician...." he began.

But Lizzie interrupted him, "No! That's what was funny, I knew there was something wrong, Old Harry couldn't have been cooking bacon sandwiches." Her voice rose with excitement as she realized what the old man had told them the day before. At long last, she knew why she didn't trust the vicar. "Because since Jennifer Lacey died of BSE....."

"He doesn't eat meat!" Tom finished the sentence for her. "So!" Tom sat back grinning as a piece of the puzzle slotted into place. "Miss Mitchell's been telling us porky pies about the bacon sandwiches!"

Lizzie sat silently going over everything that Harry had told them yesterday. A sudden rush of understanding and guilt for not realizing earlier swept over her as she remembered her brother's reply when the old man said he was a vegetarian.

"That's why Oliver said it was the living who were puzzling he knew the vicar was lying about Harry cooking meat."

"But who *was* cooking the bacon or whatever it was?" Tom asked.

"I don't know," Lizzie said. "But I know the smell was coming from underneath us yet we were on the ground floor."

Running out of space on the chalk board Tom said, "Let's have another look at Oliver's plans perhaps there's something marked on them that can help us."

Oliver's drawings were a scribbled mess and not at all easy to follow. But now that they studied them closely Tom and Lizzie could make out what seemed to be a long room that ran under the whole house.

When they had got used to Oliver's "artwork" they discovered that what they thought was a crossing out was in fact a stairway leading to this cellar from the library. That same dusty, dirty library they'd sat in just a few days before.

"This can't be right," Lizzie said puzzled. "There wasn't a staircase in that room was there? We'd have noticed it if there were wouldn't we?"

"There wasn't and we would 'ave," Tom told her. "But, suppose," he went on almost to himself, "Suppose there was a secret stairway. It's an old house and they always used to have secret passageways and rooms to hide smugglers and priests and stuff."

"Right," Lizzie said. "I'm going back there to look for Oliver. I'll break in if necessary. You'd better wait here and let the police know if I don't come back." She stood up to leave. Tom knew by the look on her face there was no use arguing with her. But he wasn't going to let her go on her own.

"Okay, okay," he said. "Let's do this properly. We'll go during the evening service when the vicar will be busy. We'll need dark clothing so we're not spotted breaking in and we'll need a torch. I'll tell my parents we're going to yours and you tell yours you'll be here, so they don't worry. We'd better leave a note somewhere though just in case we never return!"

Lizzie didn't protest about him going with her. She did not like lying to her parents but her mum, busy weeding in the garden and her dad, doing his jigsaw puzzle didn't notice her when she went back to get changed. She left two notes as arranged, with the false one on top of the truthful one, before slipping quietly out of her front door to wait for Tom.

Pacing up and down outside his house she thought back to earlier in the day when she'd complained about being tired of caring for Oliver. She would give anything now to see him turn round the corner of their street and she prayed that if he did she would never moan about him again.

But Oliver did not appear. Instead Tom's dad startled her as his figure loomed suddenly at the window. Lizzie heard him mutter, "Blooming weather!" as he closed the curtains to shut out the approaching storm. Although it was mid summer the sky was darkening early and heavy threatening clouds gathered overhead. Just as Tom was creeping out of the front door, and Rusty his dog was creeping behind the sofa shivering, the first drum rolls of thunder could be heard rumbling in the distance.

Chapter ten.

The library holds a story.

The two friends slipped like shadows through the iron gates at the top of the vicarage driveway. They skirted in and out of the bushes so they wouldn't be seen by anybody watching from the windows.

The thunder roared louder now and Lizzie worried that a bolt of lightening would flash and light them up as they scurried through the shrubbery. Working their way towards the building she felt sure unseen eyes must be watching them and although the lightening held off a quiver of electricity ran up and down her spine.

In the darkening twilight the grim, forbidding old house looked even more menacing and uninviting than in the daytime. Not one of the windows was lit and the closer they got the more the building towered over them like a monstrous giant out of a children's fairy tale. Lizzie stuck close to Tom feeling very glad he had gone with her.

They didn't want to use the front door as they were sure it would be locked so using hand signals and whispers they agreed to see if there was a window open at the back. Creeping round to the rear of the vicarage Lizzie's heart drummed so hard against her chest she was sure anyone nearby must hear it.

As they edged silently along the wall of the building the heavens opened and rain began to fall, heavier and heavier, sticking their clothes to their bodies like cling-film round meat.

The windows here were even higher than at the front and protected by black iron railings so breaking in was not an option. Suddenly Tom stifled a cry as his toe stubbed against something hard. Stumbling up a step they found themselves standing in front of an old weathered door with green paint peeling off in great flakes.

There was no way of knowing what was on the other side but this was their only chance of getting in and if they didn't get out of the rain soon they would have to give up and go home. Tom tried the handle. It turned easily enough and to their surprise the door gave a little as he pushed it. Then it stopped as if stuck on something. Tom

put his weight behind it and taking a chance the storm would drown
out any noise he shoved hard at the door. It moved jerkily inwards, its
bottom edge scraping along uneven flagstone flooring.

Tom peered around the edge of the door before stepping inside
safe at last from the wind and rain. Lizzie, following behind him,
shone the torch around a room that must be the kitchen. The beam lit
up an enormous white sink that was piled high with cups, dishes and
saucepans. A filthy cooker stood next to the sink and that too was
piled with yet more unwashed cookware. An electrical hum came from
a chest freezer against the far wall and even in the dim torchlight they
could easily make out the dirty hand prints that covered its once white
surface.

The only other furniture was a chair wedged under a table.
Someone had sat and smoked here leaving spilt ash and cigarette ends
stubbed out on the wooden top. Chipped, cracked china bowls with the
dregs of tea and cereals mixed together littered the table and a stack of
glasses balanced like a circus act. Shelves lining the third wall held
piles of packets and tinned food. Some looked familiar to the children
but others had such strange markings and labels they could not begin
to guess what they were.

They tiptoed over to a hook on the far wall where a grubby,
grey towel hung and tried to dry themselves on the filthy cloth. When
they weren't quite so wet they made their way through a door that led
out into a passage. Although they knew they were in the hallway they
could not decide which of the many identical doors led to the library.

"For goodness sake gimme that!" Tom hissed snatching the
torch out of Lizzie's hand. He focused the beam on each of the door
handles in turn. When it came to rest on the round dull brass knob he
nodded and pointing whispered, "That's the one."

They crept across the hall. After a moment's hesitation Tom
pushed open the door flinching as the rusty hinges squealed in protest.
He needn't have worried for the storm covered any noise they made.
Lizzie closed the door behind them as they entered the library.

The dark panelled walls of the gloomy room made it difficult
to see and the light from the torch didn't seem quite so bright in here.
Tom pulled the thick red velvet curtains across the windows while

Lizzie turned on a shaded table lamp and laid Oliver's plan in its pool of light. They could work out where the stairs should be but there was no sign of them in the room or that they had ever been there.

Testing out Tom's idea they worked their way round the walls pushing every panel to see if any would swing open to reveal a secret entrance. They moved aside all the pictures and searched behind each one looking for a button to press or a rope to pull. They forgot their caution and stamped on floorboards listening for any changes in the sound they made.

But there was nothing and after half an hour Tom sat down in the armchair saying, "This is pointless. We're getting nowhere."

"I'm going to see if I can find the original plan that Oliver copied, perhaps he made a mistake," said Lizzie, shining the torch around the walls to help her see in the poor light from the lamp.

"Or perhaps the stairs have been removed," Tom sighed.

As Lizzie groped her way around the room she suddenly cried out.

"What's the matter?" Tom asked leaping to his feet.

"Ugh! These cobwebs are everywhere!" spat Lizzie. "One just went in my mouth!"

Pulling the sticky threads off her tongue she continued to search the framed parchments looking for the right map.

Suddenly Tom cried out, "That's it! Don't you see? The cobwebs! The cobwebs!"

Lizzie had no idea what he was babbling on about and told him so. Cross with his stupid behaviour and still trying to rid her mouth of the taste of the spider's silk she snapped, "What are you talking about?"

"Don't you see?" Tom said again. "Why'd it be the only thing in here that doesn't have any cobwebs? Unless… It's the only thing that's always being moved!"

As he spoke he picked his way across the room, stepping over the tray of glasses and plate of biscuits that had been left lying on the floor from their last visit. When he got over to the trophy of the deer with its sad, glass eyes staring bleakly ahead he reached up and felt carefully all over the antler that Oliver had noticed. Lizzie joined him but even standing on tiptoe she was much shorter than Tom so she stepped back and let him carry on.

After several taps and tugs he tried turning the left antler. He felt it give slightly in his hand so he pushed harder half expecting it to snap and break off. Instead the whole antler suddenly twisted round in an anti-clockwise direction until it clicked to a halt.

A low grinding sound came from the wall beside them followed by the clank of a chain. Immediately like the lift doors in a department store a whole section of the wooden panelling slid apart showing a flight of stairs the other side.

"Wow!" was all Lizzie could manage to say. Tom seized the torch out of her hand and was quickly inside the secret entrance shining it into the darkness. They couldn't see past the first four steps of the wooden stairway that spiralled downwards because the rest wound out of sight round a bend.

Tom peered down but Lizzie jumped back when a damp, musty stench came up to meet them. Covering her nose with her hand she stammered, "D'you think we should go down? Or…. shall we go back and get someone?"

"You go back," Tom said. "If I'm not home in half an hour send for help."

Lizzie hesitated for only a moment. She'd been glad Tom had been with her earlier and she wasn't about to leave him on his own to fend for himself against whoever or whatever lurked below.

"We'll go together," she said in a voice that gave no hint of the fear she felt.

She followed Tom over the small step of the panelling into the dark void on the other side. Her legs began to shake and she put her hand against the wall for support but the cold, wet stone felt slimy to her touch and she pulled it away again quickly. Then forcing herself to be braver than she really was she followed Tom down the winding stairway.

Chapter eleven.

An instrument of torture.

Tom shone the feeble light from the torch onto each step. With no handrail or guide rope it would have been easy to lose their footing. So they trod slowly and carefully in the worn grooves made by the generations of people who'd passed before them.

At the bottom there was no longer any sound of the storm and it was even darker than upstairs. Tom shone the torch around and in the batteries' dying moments they glimpsed a small windowless room with shelves filled with more cartons and tins of groceries. Wooden crates and cardboard boxes were stacked from floor to ceiling and for a second Lizzie wondered if Mrs. Dale hoarded the shop's supplies here. But the strong mouldy smell and an instinctive fear told her this was no ordinary storeroom and they should get as far away from this place as possible. But even though her heart was racing she followed Tom who was feeling his way in the dark to the other side of the room.

"I think I saw a door here," Tom said. It was too dark to see anything now so Tom did not notice Lizzie jump when a wailing sound came from the other side of the wall. Tom carried on fumbling about searching for an entrance and ignored the strange noise.

"What *is* that?" Lizzie stuttered between clenched teeth. The temperature had dropped a lot but her teeth were not chattering from the cold.

Tom didn't answer at first but once he'd found the doorway he laughed replying, "It's alright. It's not some instrument of torture. I think it's a clarinet. I wanted one for Christmas once but I got a recorder instead."

Lizzie could not believe her ears as she heard a different instrument start to play. This time it was a much brighter piece of music. There was the sound of singing and clapping as well.

"It sounds like a party! Who on earth would hold one here?" she said.

"Does seem the wrong time of year for the W.I. Christmas party," Tom said. He was puzzled too and although he put out his hand to open the door he stopped as if not sure what to do next.

"You coming?" he asked Lizzie. But instead of charging ahead to look for Oliver Lizzie's confidence left her again.

"I don't know," she replied, "Who do you think's in there?"

"Let's find out, shall we?" said an icy voice behind them. "You're going to be joining them anyway!"

The two friends spun round. There on the bottom step of the stairway, lit by the flicker of the candle in her hand, was the vicar.

Robed in her black cassock she was a frightening figure. Her eyes glared at the children who froze unable to speak.

"I heard your brother had stumbled into the middle of all this," she hissed at Lizzie. "I didn't realize you wanted to make it a family get together!"

Lizzie tried to apologize for intruding but before she could stammer out two words the vicar interrupted her.

"You stupid, meddling children! You've poked your noses in too far this time!" Swooping past them like the evil queen in a fairytale she flung open the low door.

The sight in front of them was astonishing. A huge, cavernous, candlelit room crowded full of people. Their ages ranged from tiny babies in their mothers' arms to wrinkled old men. Down the middle of the room stood long trestle tables loaded with dishes of food that looked and smelt spicy and delicious: steaming casseroles, enormous pies, long kebabs and nut covered cakes. No peanut butter sandwiches or crisps at this party.

In the middle of it all, tapping his foot in time to the music and tucking into a huge sausage, sat Oliver. A very grubby Oliver with his face covered in black smudges, his hair sticking up and his clothes smeared with great dirty streaks. An old woman with a bright red knitted shawl round her shoulders squatted next to him frying more sausages over a camping stove. Teenage girls in brightly coloured dresses danced in the middle of the room. Older women sat clapping and stamping in time to the music which a young man was playing on an instrument that looked like a violin.

One by one the people in the room turned to stare at the trio in the doorway. Only Oliver and the musician, whose eyes never left the dancers, were unaware of them. As everybody else froze the fiddler's bow flew. Faster and faster, wilder and wilder. Even after the last girl had stopped dancing the lovesick violinist played on, carried away by his imagination and his music. At last he too snapped out of his trance. The tune stopped but Oliver continued to tuck into his supper.

The vicar began shrieking in a language that neither Lizzie nor Tom had ever heard before. As she did any of the people who were standing sat down on the floor like a well-disciplined school assembly. Miss Mitchell shoved the two children over towards Oliver who, after all they'd been through to find him, muttered a simple, "Oh hi," when he saw them.

The vicar pointed at the young man who had been playing the violin and spat strange words out at him. Lizzie knew by her tone of voice she was not happy. The musician hung his head in disgrace shuffling from foot to foot as though he had been told off for swearing by an elderly aunt. He slowly moved the violin and its bow behind his back hiding the instrument from the woman's sight. The vicar shifted her gaze to take in the entire roomful of people and continued to shriek fluently in a foreign language. Nobody spoke until she pointed towards the three children screaming something that Lizzie knew was about them.

At this point a large bearded man got to his feet and started to speak. But marching over to him the vicar cut him off in a voice so chilling an icy shiver ran down Lizzie's spine.

Ignoring all this and with his sausage finished Oliver picked up a slice of dark bread with some sort of meaty paste spread on it. He took one mouthful and screwing up his face in disgust spat it out on the floor wiping his tongue on his sleeve to rid himself of the taste.

Miss Mitchell, having finished scolding, swept past the children on her way out. Stepping on the mushy contents of Oliver's mouth her foot shot out from under her and with a squawk she landed flat on her back like a circus clown, the lit candle held out at arm's length. She lay perfectly still at Oliver's feet as if trying to decide which bones she had broken. Everyone held their breath.

Oliver, looking down at the fallen vicar, said, "Oops! Careful!"

No one rushed to help the vicar as she slowly stood up. Once she seemed sure she had done no real damage she flounced out of the door slamming it behind her. In the silence that followed the only sounds to be heard in the room were a key turning in the lock and bolts being slid shut. Several moments passed before people started to move and huddle together in small groups muttering to one another.

Lizzie, not wanting to frighten Oliver, lowered her voice and asked Tom, "What's going on? Who are these people?"

"I don't know," Tom whispered in reply. "But I don't think they're the Women's Institute."

"They're aliens." Oliver informed them, cramming food into his mouth as he spoke. "And you needn't whisper they can't understand you."

"Oh yes," Lizzie knew what he meant. "They're immigrants. Like the refugees we see on the TV every night."

"I think by the look of things they're more likely to be illegal immigrants than refugees," said Tom.

They'd all seen the pictures on the news each evening of people trying to find ways to get through the Channel Tunnel and smuggle themselves into Britain. Night after night they'd watched images of young men racing along train tracks, throwing themselves onto wagons or hiding in lorries, hoping to reach England to start a new life. Some even tried to row across the Channel, the treacherous stretch of watery motorway which carried a constant traffic of huge ferries. And just as a child's pedal car would fare on the M1 so the rubber dinghies they used were often found shredded and destroyed when they washed up on French or British shores with no sign of their passengers.

But here in this sanctuary in the middle of England were not just fit young men but whole families including babies, children, parents and grandparents. They could have been any group of friends or relatives on a Sunday school picnic. However Lizzie was not sure how friendly the group would be towards them especially after the vicar's speech.

She was thinking about whether they should go up to any of the foreigners when a scuffling broke out in a corner of the room. The musician and another young man, who had a dark scar running down his cheek, started pushing each other, squabbling and sparring like boys in a playground. Suddenly the man with the scar pulled a knife out from the inside of his boot and waved the gleaming blade in front of the other's face as if taunting him with it. The gigantic man who'd challenged the vicar earlier jumped up and stomped over towards the dueling pair.

In the space where he had been sitting Lizzie could see a blue, green and red checked blanket spread out over the floor. Curled up on it lay a pure white dog with long fluffy fur. She would have loved to have gone over and petted the dozing animal but the fight that was breaking out seemed so terrifying she didn't dare.

The dog's owner thrust his dark, bearded face in front of the man with the knife blocking his view of his opponent. He wrapped his huge arms around the troublemaker in a bear hug and picked him up as if he were a two-year-old toddler throwing a tantrum. Carrying him over to a corner of the room the large man threw the younger one down in a heap on the floor. The knife clattered away to land beside an old woman who sat quietly sewing. Without missing a stitch her foot shot out and slid the weapon beneath the folds of her pleated skirt where it disappeared before its owner could spot that it had gone.

The crisis seemed to have broken the spell that the vicar had cast over the group and they relaxed again and laughed at the antics of the quarrelsome duo. The dancing girls surrounded the musician who blushed as they giggled and teased him. They wouldn't leave him alone until he pulled a mouth organ out of his pocket and started playing another tune. Only the man with the scar still seemed to be smouldering with anger as he sloped off back to his group rubbing his bruised bottom. He glanced in the children's direction giving them a glare that made Lizzie shiver with fear.

Chapter twelve.

Stranger and stranger.

Lizzie took several long, deep breaths to help her calm down. The scene that had just unfolded in front of them didn't seem to have bothered anyone else but her. Even Oliver who didn't usually like large gatherings was at ease. At Christmas time he'd retreat to his bedroom to escape visiting relatives. But here, where he understood nobody and nobody understood him, he sat untroubled amongst complete strangers. He picked up another sausage from the plate the woman held out to them but changed his mind and put it back for one that wasn't, "too burnt!"

Lizzie smiled as she remembered the time Grandma Pickles told Oliver she'd give him fifty pence in exchange for a kiss. Oliver had replied that he already had fifty pence of his own and didn't want to kiss her bristly old chin. Poor Grandma never asked him again but she'd bought a pair of tweezers. Now as she looked at her younger brother Lizzie realized how much she loved him and his blunt honesty. She felt very glad to have found him here safe and sound.

Studying him she became aware how dirty he was and it dawned on her they had no idea how he'd got there. "So what've you been doing Oliver?" she asked. "What've you been up to?"

"I've been asleep," he said.

Knowing that Oliver never slept more than a few hours at night Lizzie found this very hard to believe. Even though he'd got up earlier than usual that morning she still didn't think he would have taken a nap to make up for it. After a busy day, or even if he was ill, when anyone else would have been falling asleep on their feet, Oliver would still be going strong. She couldn't believe that he had suddenly changed and started taking siestas.

Tom, who up until now had been busy watching the refugees, tried to help Lizzie question her brother.

"What time did you leave the park Oliver and why did you leave?"

Lizzie thought he sounded more like a police officer than a friend. She wondered if he was secretly enjoying all the drama with the vicar and this strange group of people. He always said he wanted to be a detective and he certainly seemed to be playing the role now.

But Oliver was not an easy witness to interrogate. "How should I know what time it was. It was time to get my video."

"What video?" Lizzie asked.

Before he had a chance to reply Tom took over again. "Why did you come here Oliver?" he asked.

"To get my video," Oliver said again.

"But there aren't any of your videos here," Tom said.

Oliver snapped back, "It *is* my video, so there!"

Lizzie could see they were not getting anywhere so to calm things down she said, "It's okay, we just wanted to know what made you come here and what happened to you."

Oliver raised his eyes as if to say, "Why don't you listen?"

Very slowly and deliberately, as if he were talking to a pair of five year olds Oliver repeated, "I....came....to....get....my....vid...e...o. Then I slid down the policeman's slide."

"Oh shut up Oliver," Tom said. Turning to Lizzie he asked, "What's he talking about?"

"I have no idea," Lizzie answered.

Before they could ask him anything more a group of men in a corner of the room began shouting and arguing with one another. The gang pointed towards the three children. One of the men got up and began waving his arms around and Lizzie felt sure they were all going to be murdered. After a few minutes the big man, who had stopped the fight earlier, stood up and strode over to the door. He tried turning the handle, twisting and yanking at it, but nothing happened. The entrance had been locked and was not going to open. Even when he put his massive shoulder against it and shoved with all his strength the centuries old, solid wood door held fast. This part of the building had been designed as a fortress and the sixteenth century builders had done a good job.

The man lumbered back to his noisy, restless companions and stood in front of them like Mrs. Williams waiting for silence before starting a lesson. Eventually the hubbub stopped and everyone settled down and gave him their attention.

Lizzie could not understand a word he said. But even though the foreigners often turned round and glanced at her and the boys while he spoke she felt they no longer had anything to fear.

When he had finished talking there was a general murmur of agreement and as the women returned to their chores many of the men went over to the speaker and clapped him on the back. Then the man hoisted himself up and ambled over to the three children.

In slow, stumbling English he said, "I am sorry. This is er… difficult for you. It is difficult for us also. We not want er…. problems for you. Your English woman is a problem. She is bad. Very bad. But we help you. We leave here together. Okay?"

"I'm Tom," Tom told the man. "And this is Lizzie and Oliver. What's your name?"

"You not say my name," the man's voice rumbled as he laughed. "What you want call me?"

"Big Bear," Lizzie blurted out without a seconds thought.

He rumbled with laughter again. "Okay Big Bear find way out. No problem."

Lizzie feeling quite brave now said, "Can we see your dog please?"

The man grinned, "Okay. Yes. You come see my dog."

He hauled himself up and steered Lizzie and the boys over to the rug. The crowd round it moved to one side so they could get a better look.

"Oh!" said Tom.

"Aah!" said Lizzie.

"Ooh!" said Oliver.

For the dog was not lying asleep as they had thought but was on her side feeding two beautiful, snow white puppies. They were making contented little mewing sounds as they suckled.

"They're so lovely!" Lizzie managed to say when she'd got her breath back.

"Yes, they are …. *loverly*," Big Bear repeated the word as if it was new to him. "But I not know she have babies. Now I must help them also."

Lizzie looked up at his face surprised to see tears well up in his gentle, grey eyes. She knew here was someone who really understood what caring felt like. He blinked back the tears and ruffling Oliver's hair he motioned them back to their places saying, "Okay. Now Big Bear find way out."

Sitting back down Tom looked round the room and said, "I don't see how we are going to get out of here. There are no windows and the only door's the one we came through."

"Won't there be another secret door?" Lizzie asked. "After all if a priest came down here to escape he'd need a way out wouldn't he?"

"Doubt it," Tom said dashing her hopes. "They'd just hole up here till the coast was clear and then when whoever was looking for them had gone they'd go back up."

"Then we're trapped!" Lizzie cried.

Chapter thirteen.

The great escape.

"I wonder why Miss Mitchell's shut everybody in this cellar," Tom said. "I wonder what she's up to."

"I don't know," Lizzie's voice shook as she spoke. "Or what she's planning to do to us. Oh we have to find a way out!"

"We could go up the slide," Oliver said.

"What slide?" Lizzie asked puzzled.

"The policeman's slide," Oliver answered.

Tom was beginning to shake his head so Oliver jumped up and pulled Lizzie over to a dark corner at the end of the room.

"There!"

Her brother pointed to a sturdy little wooden cupboard about the height of Tom's waist. It was a roughly made piece of furniture covered with black smudge marks and dents. It did not seem to be anything out of the ordinary except that it was built onto the wall.

Tom pulled the door but instead of it opening sideways as expected it dropped down and hung open like a jaw. There was a three-sided metal bucket attached to the door which slotted back up into the cupboard when it was shut. Instead of a back panel there was a metal scoop at the base of the bucket that stuck out into a deep hole.

Tom peered inside twisting his body to try to see. There was too little light down this end of the room so Lizzie fetched a candle and he tried again. Ignoring the pain from the hot wax that was dripping onto his fingers he held the candle in one hand and pulled himself into the bucket with the other. His body twisted and turned as he pulled with his arm and pushed with his feet until suddenly he shot out of sight. Lizzie waited not sure what to do.

Just as she was convinced something dreadful must have happened to Tom she heard him coughing and spluttering before his head popped out above the cupboard door. Chuckling he announced, "It's a coal cellar. And guess what? Oliver's right. Only there isn't a policeman's slide but a coal man's chute. And I think it leads to the outside!"

His long legs made it as difficult climbing out as it was climbing in but having left the candle inside he could use both arms to help him this time. He told them that there was a space built into the wall behind the cupboard which had been used for storing coal. The cupboard was where in the old days servants would have come to take the coal from.

"The coalman would've emptied sacks of coal down the chute from the outside," he told Lizzie. "That way he didn't have to drag dirt through the house. There are shutters at the top. I can't open them but we might be able to get out through them. There are still a few lumps of coal left in there, it's very dirty."

By this time a small, noisy crowd had gathered around the children and they were jostled out of the way as people examined their discovery.

Big Bear was called over and once he had seen the find for himself he huddled together with a group of his men. Then they rushed back to their families and the room buzzed with activity like an organized beehive. The women cleared away food, collected their cooking equipment and packed up belongings. A group of men pulled the doors off and the cupboard was taken apart. Within two minutes, using just their hands and feet, they'd enlarged the hole in the wall where the cupboard had been so that even Big Bear could pass through easily.

Before the children had time to realize what was happening Lizzie, Tom and Oliver found themselves being herded along with other children and their families. They were dragged into the dusty space in the wall then pushed and shoved by strong arms up a narrow metal ramp. The shutters stood kicked open and like a chimney sweep's brush they were each shot out, covered in soot, into the welcoming storm that continued to rage outside.

There was no time for saying thank you or goodbye. Their fellow captives poured out of the underground prison. They pulled shawls and jackets over their heads before the black shadows of the vicarage garden swallowed them up. Lizzie thought she caught a glimpse of Big Bear. His coat was pulled round a bundle that was clutched to his chest and the pale shape of a dog trotted along beside him. But he vanished before she had time to call out.

A sudden flash of lightning lit the children like actors standing in a spotlight on a stage.

"Come on," Tom said, "Let's get out of here."

The three of them ran as fast as they could. Oliver did his best not to get left behind. He flung his arms round madly as he tried to stay upright on the wet grass. Once they were well clear of the building and in the shadow and shelter of the bushes they stopped to catch their breath.

"What shall we do?" Lizzie panted. "We'd better go home and ring the police hadn't we?"

"If we waste time that woman's going to get away." Tom said meaning the vicar. "If we can take the back lane it goes straight past P.C. Pane's house. He's bound to be in, it's Sunday evening. If he isn't we can call the police from the phone-box on the corner of his street."

"Shouldn't we just go straight home?" Lizzie begged, she'd had enough of playing detective.

But Tom was in charge. "No. It won't take any longer going the back way and if P.C. Pane's there he'll get things moving quicker than us. It can take forever before they answer a 999 call."

They set out on the pebbly little footpath that passed the back of the church en route to the police officer's road. They took no notice of the storm which raged around them. There was more than that to worry about now.

Nearing the church Lizzie felt her body stiffen. Each step she took got more and more difficult and her legs began to drag. She knew this was where the murder had happened. Saying nothing to the others as they made their way through the graveyard she forced her feet to keep moving. When they got closer to the entrance porch her imagination started to play tricks on her and the gravestone shadows seemed to change shape as if the bodies in the graves were on the move. She stopped dead in her tracks her feet rooted to the ground, unable to take another step. Tom stopped and looked at his friend. He started to move towards her but lightning slashed a jagged wound across the night sky followed immediately by such a hideous scream that he too froze.

He stood moving neither towards Lizzie nor away from her as if he did not know what to do. Lizzie grabbed Oliver by the arm and dragging him after her ran into the church.

Chapter fourteen.

A watery grave.

The three children raced into the building to discover that not all of the church goers had got home safely after the evening service.

The vicar lay over the christening font like a doll thrown out of a pram. Her long slender arms splayed out across the cold stone making Lizzie think of a puppet whose strings had been cut. Her face was submerged in the water used for baptizing babies. As the children watched she slid to the floor to lie in a crumpled heap at the base of the pedestal like last season's unwanted plaything.

Edging closer to the body Lizzie and Tom stepped over a silver candlestick.

Seeing the vicar's blue tinged face, her eyes staring wildly like the glass eyes of the deer at the vicarage, Lizzie asked, "Is she dead?"

"Of course she's dead!" Tom replied.

Lizzie her voice shaking asked, "Has she killed herself?"

Tom stared at Lizzie, "You can't hit yourself on the back of your own head!"

Lizzie, her voice rising cried, "She's been murdered?"

Oliver went over and looked closely at the vicar taking in every detail. Lizzie tried to pull him away to protect him from the horrible sight.

But, "She looks just like the dead woman in "The killer", when her body's found in the park," was all he said.

For the first time Lizzie had an idea of what life was like for her brother. Real life and fantasy had merged together and she felt as if she didn't know what was true and what wasn't. Every sight and sound was as clear as the next and nothing made sense. An angelic baby Jesus grinned down at her from a stained glass window. Pigeons beating their wings deafened her as they flew down from their perches on the rafters. The smell of mould and mildew made her feel sick.

"You alright?" Tom asked.

"Yes. I think so. Let's get out of here."

"Right," he said. "We'll go straight to P.C. Pane's."

As they turned to leave Lizzie thought she saw the curtain hanging in front of the entrance to the bell tower start to sway slightly. She wondered if she was seeing things again.

But the green folds of material continued to move. The curtains parted and the scarred man from the cellar stepped out. Lizzie wanted to scream but although she opened her mouth no sound came out.

"Run!" shouted Tom.

Her legs moved and as they ran both she and Tom grabbed hold of Oliver's arms. They dragged him down the aisle straight into Big Bear's huge arms! He lifted them up as if they weighed nothing and carried them back down the church like a newly born litter of kittens. None of the children even tried to struggle. There was no point. They were no match against his enormous strength. He sat them down on one of the pews and grinned at them.

"I am best in my country you know," he boasted.

"The best?" Tom stammered. "The best what?"

All sorts of ideas came to Lizzie's mind: robber, murderer, terrorist!

"Weight-lifter. I am strongest man in all Albania!" He flexed the muscles in his right arm.

Then as if he'd just remembered he looked sadly in the direction of the vicar and said, "Er... I'm sorry for your English lady."

Suddenly Lizzie's emotions bubbled over and she recovered her lost voice, "No you're not! You let him kill her!" she shouted pointing at the scar-faced man who was standing next to him.

To the children's immense surprise Big Bear's face creased into a smile then he roared with laughter as he cuffed the other man about the head. He looked directly at Lizzie and putting his hand over his heart he said, "You no worry about my little brother. He no hurt you. He hurt no one. He er... show off. That's all."

Gazing once more at the figure lying on the floor he said, "But this is not good news for us. We're not safe here. We must go away, far away." Adding, "I'm sorry we've put you in danger."

Big Bear spoke quickly to his brother in their own language but when he turned back towards the children it was as if he were a different person. He scowled at all of them in turn, his finger stabbing the air an inch away from each of their faces, as he ordered, "You. Stay here."

They were not going to argue with him but as if to make sure they got the message he bent down until the tip of his nose was touching the tip of Tom's.

"You move from here you very, very sorry!" He spat the words in the boy's face.

The children all sat bolt upright.

"You understand?" The man shouted.

They all nodded and the two men started to walk away. Before they disappeared behind the curtain Big Bear turned back towards the children and waggling his finger at them he warned, "Trust no one. Remember this, no one!"

Before the curtain closed behind him Lizzie caught sight of a long, white, fluffy tail wagging from side to side.

Tom, Lizzie and Oliver sat in stunned silence. None of them dared move or speak and all three stayed where the man had told them to. Oliver continued to sit up straight as if he were nailed to the back of the pew.

After what seemed like hours but was probably only minutes Oliver's stomach got the better of him. He started to swing his legs and clutch his tummy and groan. The sound broke Lizzie and Tom out of their trance and Lizzie said, "What's the matter, Oliver? What's wrong?"

"I'm hungry," he wailed. "Can't we go home now?"

Lizzie lost it.

"How can we go home?" She shouted at him. "Don't be so stupid! You heard what he said, we can't move! They're probably waiting outside for us right now! You never think of anyone but yourself! It's always about you and what you want! Oliver this! Oliver that! You don't care about anyone else! You're an idiot. Do you want them to get us?"

Oliver looked stunned at his sister's outburst. He stopped moving his legs and stared at her. Lizzie never shouted. When Oliver had first learnt to use scissors and cut all the hair off her favourite doll,

Beauty Golden, Lizzie had been the one to calm their mum down. Now she was screaming at him and she couldn't stop.

Oliver didn't cry. He hadn't cried since he was a baby. He had tantrums and got cross and frustrated, but he had not cried real tears for as long as anyone could remember. Now, his face reddened, his chin quivered and his bottom lip trembled. But he didn't cry. When Lizzie saw what she had done she jumped off the pew and raced over to him slinging her arms round his neck. "I'm so sorry," she cried. "I didn't mean it."

That changed everything.

Oliver pushed her away saying, "I'm not stupid. I'm not an idiot. I was only thinking that Mum would have tea ready and we shouldn't be late."

Before either of them could say any more Tom said, "Shush! Shut up Oliver! Listen, the pair of you! Can't you hear that?"

The brother and sister tilted their heads and listened. It was faint at first. But it got louder and louder.

As the thunderclouds rolled away a fleet of wailing vehicles rolled to a halt in front of the entrance to the church. There were at least six police cars as well as two ambulances. Blue lights flashed and sirens shrieked as more than a dozen pairs of black boots stormed in to rescue the children.

That night, after the police had asked them a few questions, the children were sent home and a doctor called to check them over. Dr Bell told the children she was going to retire soon as she was very old. Oliver said he knew she was old because her hair was so grey. Dr Bell smiled and this made little wrinkles round her eyes. She chatted to the children right up until bedtime when she said that they all seemed fine after their adventure.

She did say that she would make a date for Oliver and Mr. and Mrs. Pickles to see a doctor she knew at Leicester hospital.

She left some medicine for the three youngsters in case they couldn't sleep but they didn't go to bed before finding out that although

74

Lizzie's parents had found her notes they were not the ones who had first called the police. A man with a foreign accent had rung the emergency services to say there had been a murder and three children were in great danger.

Chapter fifteen.

Oliver's got a complaint.

Over the next few days Lizzie and Tom told the police, and the stream of visitors who dropped by with cards and gifts, everything that had happened.

In the middle of all the excitement the hospital doctor shocked Mr. and Mrs. Pickles by telling them that Oliver had Asperger's Syndrome and that was why he behaved as he did. Over the days and weeks that followed Oliver and his family were given support and advice and as everybody else learnt to deal with his condition Oliver became less of a problem.

It did mean however that his teachers had some homework to do as they knew little about Asperger's Syndrome.

Mr. Jones turned up one day with a present for Oliver, a football magazine. He remembered as he handed it to his pupil that Oliver did not like the game. His visit lasted no more than a quarter of an hour but to Lizzie it dragged on like the time they'd spent trapped in Doreen's greenhouse. The teacher struggled to find anything to say to the children. He told them about his short holiday that he was planning to take in Devon.

Then he remembered that there was another place he had to be and trying to find something to say as he was leaving he said, "Well Oliver, seems we've found a sport you can manage after all!" Oliver stared at him.

"Sledging!" Mr. Jones whooped in delight at his own joke as he made a swooping gesture with his hand to represent Oliver sliding down the coal chute. "Only without the sledge!" he finished laughing as he opened the door to let himself out.

Unfortunately he didn't notice the doormat was jammed in the bottom of the door and his foot caught in the matting. Mr. Jones fell headlong out of the front doorway landing on the gravel path outside. Lizzie helped him back onto his feet but as she brushed the dirt off his sleeve she was sure she heard Oliver calling, "Have a nice trip."

The police did not bother Oliver with too many questions and they tried to shield him and the two families from the press. An officer or "minder," as Tom called the woman police officer stood at the end of their road and all visitors to the street were vetted as once more the news crews camped out on the village green. Old Harry was a celebrity again and even their neighbour Doreen had to pelt reporters with her home-made rock cakes as they chased after her when she visited the children.

The whole village buzzed with gossip about the dreadful affair and Mrs. Dale was kept busier than ever supplying not only stamps and groceries but all the latest news to anyone who entered her shop.

The youngsters tried to hide from all the fuss by spending as much time as possible down their den reading the newspapers and going over all the police reports they could find. One day, in the last week of August as the end of their holidays grew near they noticed that someone had been using their private hideaway. They found partly burnt twigs and ash and charcoal, all the signs that a small fire had been lit down there recently and extra large chicken or turkey bones lay strewn around.

Worse still, instead of the sweet musky scent of foxes that usually came to greet them, they were met by the stench of tobacco.

"Those lads from the end house must be coming down here to smoke so their mum doesn't catch them," said Tom. "They've no right, this is private property."

As they sat in their lair moaning about their neighbours Oliver dragged a twig through the soft earth marking out endless figure eight shapes. The stick caught on something in the ground and Oliver dug around with his fingers until he had unearthed it.

"What's that?" Lizzie asked.

"Nothing," he replied quickly hiding whatever it was in his trouser pocket before his sister could see what he'd found.

"Come on, what was it?" Lizzie tried to tug his hand out of his pocket but he pulled away from her.

"It's nothing," Oliver squealed again.

"Oh shut up Oliver and you too Lizzie," Tom snapped. "I'm trying to read this article about Miss Mitchell. Apparently she'd been secretly working with a gang of people smugglers bringing illegal immigrants into Britain from Albania."

"How could she get away with it though?" Lizzie said.

"Well," Tom looked up from the newspaper. "She was forever collecting money and clothes and stuff for her Sending Care and Miracles charity. And everybody got used to her doing wacky things so nobody ever questioned the trips she used to make. Most of the villagers helped her in one way or another. In fact Dad's just told me he was actually thinking of driving one of the vans next time she went abroad. She was always looking for volunteers."

"But how could she smuggle people into England?" Lizzie asked. "Mum said she's smuggled quite a few in. I still don't understand how she did it."

"She used to bring them in as charity workers," Tom explained. "Somehow she got hold of forged papers and used the cover of the Church to find work for them."

"How was she going to find work for that lot we saw, all those kids and old grannies?" Lizzie said.

"Who knows. They've arrested some of her contacts from abroad but nobody has any information about who she worked with in this country. She couldn't have been working alone though. They've rounded up most of the people from the cellar but they haven't found Big Bear and he was the only one who spoke English and who knew Miss Mitchell."

"Did she murder the man in the graveyard?" Lizzie asked.

"P.C. Pane thinks he was killed by one of the immigrants." Tom told her. "But Mrs. Dale says they all thought he'd been moved to his new home in Scotland. They didn't know he was dead."

"So who killed Miss Mitchell?" Lizzie asked.

"Nobody knows," Tom said. "But Big Bear and his brother are the most likely suspects. Don't forget Scar-Face did attack the musician with a knife."

The children read the newspaper articles about themselves and how they had *endured horrendous suffering,* at the hands of the *cut-throat Barbarians.*

None of the children felt that they had been "brave" or "heroic," but it did make Lizzie feel uneasy when she thought about Oliver sitting in the middle of these "barbarians" as their party guest.

At that moment Mrs. Pickles called, "Lizzie, Oliver, Tom, P.C. Pane's here to see you."

He had made it his duty to befriend the youngsters and would often arrive on their doorstep like a favourite uncle with presents for them all. He even remembered Mr. Pickle's love of jigsaw puzzles. But Oliver especially he showered with gifts although most weren't to the boy's taste and they lay ignored on the kitchen dresser.

They scrambled up the bank to meet him but Tom rushed back towards his own house shouting over his shoulder as he went,

"I'll catch you up. I'm writing a letter to find out what I need to do to join the police force. I'll go and fetch it so P.C. Pane can look it over for me."

♣

The policeman looked up and beamed when Lizzie and Oliver ran into the living room. He held out a video that he had brought round for Oliver, a wildlife documentary about dolphins.

But instead of taking the present Oliver folded his arms and turned huffily away from the man. P.C. Pane knew the boy didn't always look directly at people when he was talking to them so he didn't heed the warning signs. Pushing the video towards Oliver and thrusting it into his hands he said,

"I'm sure you'll love this one, it even shows a baby dolphin being born."

Oliver raised his arm and threw the plastic box back at the policeman so that it caught him painfully on the side of his face.

"Don't want it now," he shouted.

The officer rubbed his stinging cheek and stared at the boy open mouthed.

Lizzie was shocked at her brother's tantrum.

"Oliver! Don't be so rude! Say you're sorry to P.C. Pane at once. He's been really kind to us. Why are you being so awful?"

"I don't want his rotten old video now!" Oliver shouted back at her. "I didn't want it in the first place. I've got plenty of videos about dolphins. I didn't want to go down that slide. He hurt my head!"

The policeman's face turned bright red. Mrs. Pickles ran out of the kitchen where she had been making their visitor a cup of tea. She stood in front of Oliver and wagged her finger at him.

"Oliver how dare you be so rude! I'm appalled at you! Go to your room at once! Go on! Now! This minute!" she shouted as Oliver didn't seem to be moving.

The boy stormed out of the room without another word and slammed the door behind him so that the windowpanes rattled. He stomped up the stairs to his bedroom.

His mother tried to apologize to the officer explaining how even though they now had the diagnosis of autism it still didn't mean that Oliver was ever going to be cured. But the man didn't wait to hear what Mrs. Pickles had learnt about the "complex condition" from the leaflets she'd been given.

After she'd let him out of the front door Lizzie's mum went back to her chores in the kitchen so she did not see the look of horror on her daughter's face.

Chapter sixteen.

The long arm of the criminal.

Lizzie raced round to Tom's house next door. His mum was baby sitting his young cousins and Lizzie found her friend hastily rewriting his letter to the police because the "Dastardly Duo" had drawn all over. The toddlers followed Tom and Lizzie everywhere they went and there was nowhere in his house they could talk in private.

"We must talk it's urgent," whispered Lizzie prising a three year old off her arm. "I'll go back and get Oliver," she said. "You sneak out and meet us down the banks in two minutes."

She ran back home again and dashed in to the kitchen. She knew she would have to sweet talk her mum into reducing Oliver's sentence.

"You remember what that nice lady from the National Autistic Society said Mum?" she began. "Stick to the rules and keep tasks short and manageable. Well, you've stuck to the rules, you've punished him. I don't think you should keep the punishment up for too long or he won't remember what he's being punished for."

"But it's only been two minutes," her mum began. Seeing the look of concern on her daughter's face she relented saying, "You're a big softie, you are. Go on then, let the prisoner go. Though I'll be blowed if I know what's got into him today."

That was the easy part. It was harder snapping Oliver out of his temper as he sat hunched up, his arms crossed, on the end of his bed. Lizzie had to bribe him with an ice cream picnic to coax him out of his bedroom.

*

When Tom joined them in their hidey-hole he glanced back over his shoulder before taking the ice cream cone that Lizzie held out to him.

"I've a feeling I'm being followed, but I can't see anyone. If those "rug-rats" find out about our den we'll never get any peace from them."

He stopped when he saw that Lizzie wasn't interested in his boisterous cousins, she hadn't even unwrapped her ice cream. Unlike Oliver whose mouth was already smeared with chocolate.

"What's wrong?" Tom asked his friend.

Lizzie explained about Oliver's reaction to P.C. Pane's gift.

"Well, perhaps he's gone off dolphins," Tom said. "His interests do change remember when it was all dinosaurs this and dinosaurs that? He knew the name of every flipping dinosaur there was and so did I by the time he'd finished!"

"No, listen will you!" Lizzie shouted at him. "When we were in that cellar Oliver told us he went down the policeman's slide. You corrected him and called it a coalman's chute. But why would he mention a policeman?"

"I don't know perhaps he thought a policeman used it," Tom suggested.

"Yes but why? Why would he think about a policeman?"

They both looked at Oliver who was eyeing up Lizzie's untouched ice cream.

"Oliver," Tom began, "Why did you..."

"No!" Lizzie yanked at her friend's arm before he could say anymore and pushed him away from her brother. "I'll ask him," she said.

Turning Oliver to face her Lizzie bent forward until they made eye contact. "Oliver," she began. "Do you remember when we had that picnic in the park?"

"Yes," he replied, hoping that the right answers might win him another mint and choc chip cornet.

"You were drawing," Lizzie continued. "We fell asleep."

"Yes," Oliver agreed.

"You left Tom and me, didn't you?" Tom opened his mouth to interrupt but Lizzie shushed him.

Her brother hesitated before once again answering, "Yes."

"You told me before that you went to get your video. Which video was it?"

Oliver half shut his eyes peeping out from between his lashes. Keeping his head lowered his eyes searched the ground darting from place to place as if trying to decide what it was she wanted to hear.

"Just tell me what really happened Oliver. Tell me everything. She sat back, folded her arms and waited, giving him time to make up his mind. Lizzie realized that he'd tried to tell them before and now he was deciding whether he should give them one more chance.

"I wanted my dolphin video," he explained. "I saw P.C. Pane walking past the church so I went to ask him if I could have my dolphin video. He promised he'd give it to me when he came round," he added as if they were going to tell him off for wanting it.

"It's alright Oliver just tell us what happened," Lizzie said.

"I couldn't catch up with him he was walking too fast," the boy continued. "I went after him but I couldn't catch up with him. When he got to the vicarage I ran round the back after him but he was talking to Big Bear. I waited for them to finish because you said I shouldn't but in when someone's speaking. When they saw me Big Bear went inside but P.C. Pane got really angry and kept shouting at me. He said I was spying on them. I wasn't. I was only asking him for the video. I wouldn't have asked him if I'd known he didn't want me to have it."

At last Oliver paused for breath and glanced at the melting ice cream as if worried that this admission would scupper his chances of getting it. Lizzie handed the treat to him.

He gobbled it down quickly speaking between mouthfuls.

"I must have made him really mad 'cos he shoved me backwards. I tripped over something behind me and fell down the slide and then I don't remember any more till I woke up in that cupboard. My head hurt like mad and it was so dark I thought I was dead."

Oliver winced but they didn't know if it was from the memory of hurting his head or the cold ice cream. He swallowed and carried on, "I heard voices so I pushed the door open and crawled out. Nobody saw me. I shut the door behind me and sat there for ages and ages before that lady came along and gave me a sausage to eat. Those sausages were better than Harpers weren't they?"

He smiled as he remembered the taste and Lizzie was struck with guilt when she realized how much he'd been through because of her. She'd got him involved in something very scary and she was only now realizing how dangerous it actually was.

At long last Tom also understood the meaning of what Oliver was saying and he shook his head in disbelief as he said, "So that means P.C. Pane's in on it too! Why didn't you tell all this to anyone Oliver?"

"I *tried* to tell you," he said. "But *you* didn't believe me, so why would anyone else? Besides I thought I'd get told off for upsetting P.C. Pane. I usually get the blame for everything!"

Lizzie nodded understanding at last what her brother was saying. "That'd explain why you said you'd been asleep. You must have been knocked out when you fell down the coal chute. What I don't understand though is why P.C. Pane keeps coming round to see us."

"He's keeping an eye on us to see if we're on to him I expect." said Tom. "He's waiting to see if Oliver's going to say anything."

Lizzie was starting to piece the puzzle together. "He probably thinks the blow on his head has made Oliver forget everything and he wants to know the minute he regains his memory," she said.

She thought for a while then said, "You know I liked Big Bear. I don't think he or his brother killed Miss Mitchell."

"Do you mean what I think you mean?" Tom asked. "Do you think P.C. Pane did it?"

"You remember how we were going to go to his house after the vicar was murdered and then Big Bear frightened us and made us stay in the church?" Lizzie said. "I bet Big Bear was protecting us. I bet it was him who phoned the police. He didn't want us getting killed too!"

They stared at each other. Lizzie's cheeks changed from the colour of peaches to that of paper as the blood drained from her face at the thought of the risks they had taken and the danger they were probably still in.

"We're going to have to report all this to the police," Tom said.

"Good job I'm here then," said a voice behind them. "Save you the trouble of making the journey won't it?"

Chapter seventeen.

Back to school.

The usually cheerful police officer was glaring at them his mouth distorted into a sneer. But the children weren't looking at his face they were all concentrating on the gun that he held in his right hand which was pointing straight at Tom's chest.

There was a movement on the far bank behind them, something or someone was making their way to the top. But the children did not take their eyes off the figure in front of them. He glanced in the direction the sound was coming from and, after giving a brief nod to whoever was behind them, growled at the terrified children,

"Face me. You'll do exactly what I tell you if you know what's good for you."

Dragging Lizzie and Oliver to their feet he pushed them over to stand beside Tom.

"Right," P.C. Pane continued. "Let's go for a walk. You lead the way."

He waved the weapon to show that they were to make their way down the bank and across the soft mud gully at the bottom. Then prodding Tom hard in the ribs with the gun he forced them to scramble through the thick vegetation.

It was a difficult descent for the policeman. In turn the children pinned back the brambles to pass through safely but P.C. Pane was not used to this. He wasn't ready when Oliver released the spiky whips early so they slashed and tore into his shirt and shiny new trousers. Dodging brambles and pulling his feet from the boggy patches that the children avoided made him tired and angry so he kept pushing Oliver. At last the boy tripped and something shiny and metallic fell out of his pocket. He put out his hand to pick it up but the policeman's black boot crushed down on it. When the man lifted his foot Oliver counted his fingers to make sure he still had all five.

The police officer bent down and picked the thing up eyeing it curiously. "Hello, what's this then?" he asked. Nobody knew what the strange silver object was so they couldn't help him. It was covered in bits of grass and dry leaves so to clean it out and get a better look P.C. Pane put it to his mouth and blew the debris off it.

A shiny, brown earwig crawled out of the end nearest the officer's mouth its tiny pincers nipping the man's lip as it did so. With a yelp of surprise and disgust he threw the slim tube and its occupant back down onto the ground.

"Get up there," he snarled as they made their way across the ravine before climbing the steep bank on the other side.

This was an equally difficult journey. A lot of the time they had to scramble on hands and knees and haul themselves up ledges by hanging on to roots and branches and the ropes that the older boys had tied to the trees. Eventually they reached the top and scratched, bruised and bleeding they found themselves next to the wire fence that bordered the school grounds.

They stood catching their breath while the policeman, puffing and panting pulled away a section of the netting that had been cut ready for them.

Lizzie, trying to distract the policeman and give Tom a chance to escape said, "You killed that man in the churchyard didn't you?"

Keeping the gun focused on the knot of fear that was growing in Tom's stomach P.C. Pane replied,

"He was annoying me. Just like you three are doing. The stupid kid kept sneaking out, breaking into the shops for food and cigarettes. I didn't want to do it, but when I tried to stop him he made such a fuss I had no option. He was going to give the game away. They were nothing but trouble that lot. Always making a racket with their singing and dancing."

Ignoring the danger Lizzie kept on hoping her friend would be able to make a bid for freedom. She knew that she and Oliver wouldn't get away but maybe Tom would be able to summon help before it was too late.

"You killed Miss Mitchell too didn't you?" she said.

But his answer surprised her, "No that wasn't me."

89

He didn't once take his eyes off Tom and before Lizzie could think of anything else to say he stopped her by shouting,

"Shut up, that's enough now. I don't want to hurt you. Don't make me do something I don't want to. Let's get going." Then he hurried them across the playing field towards the school building.

During the summer holidays the caretaker, who lived nearby, regularly came to mow the grass. But he was not there today and although they could hear a dog barking far away there was no one around to witness the three children being shoved through the unlocked fire door. They were pushed forward their stumbling footsteps echoing eerily along deserted corridors that were usually full of jostling, noisy pupils. They passed empty classrooms. If their teachers had they been there they would surely have rescued them but most of them were still soaking up the sun's rays on foreign beaches and could not help.

When they reached the stock cupboard door with its key in the lock the policeman held it open saying, "You shouldn't be able to get up to any mischief in here."

They trooped in meekly, too terrified to disobey. Once inside he closed and locked the door behind them and as they stood in the darkness they heard his heavy footsteps plod away into the distance.

"Quick." Tom took charge of the situation immediately. Finding the light switch he flicked it on telling his two friends to, "Look round. Find a way out."

They searched the walls, the ceiling and the floor to see if there was an escape route. The shelves were stacked high with paper of every colour and texture. There were exercise books, paints, pens, rulers, all the supplies the school would need for the coming term. But the tiny room did not hide a window or an exit of any kind.

The children dropped down on to the floor and sat slumped, the hard spines of disused textbooks digging into their backs.

"What are we going to do?" Lizzie asked Tom willing him to create a miracle.

"I don't know," he replied. "Anyway isn't it usually about this time that Oliver saves the day?"

They both looked towards Oliver but the boy was rocking back and forth his knees clasped to his chest. He wasn't going to be able to get them out this time.

Tom continued to scan the room and its contents as if looking for inspiration. "I've got an idea!" he shouted, jumping up. "If the key's still in the lock we might be able to knock it out onto a sheet of paper and drag it under the door."

"Will that work?" Lizzie asked.

"It's better than just sitting here doing nothing," Tom replied.

He knelt in front of the door and peered through the keyhole then thumped the air with his fist. "Yes!"

Lizzie could see that he was obviously delighted with his brainwave as he started yanking sheets of card off a shelf. He told her to find something, "long and thin and pointy," that they could poke the key out of the lock with.

"Will this do?" Lizzie asked, holding out a compass.

Tom snatched it out of her hand and sliding a large sheet of thin, red cardboard under the door he knelt down again and started poking and prodding the compass in the keyhole.

Oliver watched showing no sign of interest. Then, "Won't fit", he said.

Lizzie turned away from looking at what Tom was doing and silenced her brother with a, "shush."

"It does fit doesn't it Tom?" she asked.

"Shut up Oliver," Tom replied busily working away with the compass. "Got it!" he said. Then, "Oh blow!" as the compass slipped.

Tom continued struggling with the lock for several minutes until suddenly there was a clunk as the key hit the sheet of card lying waiting for it on the floor.

"At last," Tom sighed in relief and Lizzie let out the long breath she had been holding.

"Stand back," Tom ordered. "I'm going to pull the card under now."

He slowly and very gently slid the red sheet towards them, inching it carefully into the small storeroom. But when the far edge of the sheet appeared without the key on top both Lizzie and Tom realized what Oliver had known all along. The key was too big to fit under the narrow gap beneath the door.

Close to tears Lizzie sat back down while Tom stood with his forehead pressed against the door.

Several minutes passed with no one speaking.

"What's that," Tom said looking up. Footsteps trotted down the corridor. Not the heavy tread of the policeman's, these were much lighter and quicker. Lizzie sat up straight. Someone was coming to help them.

She jumped up anxious that whoever it was should not go past and leave them there. She banged her fists against the door. Tom joined her and they hollered as loudly as they could afraid the room might be soundproof.

Thankfully the person stopped outside the door and the children stood back in relief as they heard someone scrabbling on the floor to retrieve the key before unlocking the door.

Chapter eighteen.

In at the deep end.

As the door swung open Lizzie cried out in delight. Wearing a grubby trouser suit with a tear just above the knee and high heeled shoes caked in mud Mrs. Williams stood in the doorway. The girl threw herself into her kind, gentle head teacher's arms while Tom jumped up and down with excitement.

Oliver did not make any move to get up from the floor. He did not even seem to realize that help had arrived and he stayed curled up, his head tucked down on his knees. Lizzie and Tom were both speaking at once trying desperately to explain the urgency of the situation and make their teacher understand they must get away and call the police as quickly as possible.

"Oh, thank goodness it's you!" Lizzie was shouting. "It's P.C. Pane! He's one of the smugglers! He locked us in here 'cos we know too much! We've got to get away from here! He's got a gun!"

Tom was shouting over her saying, "We've got to call the police immediately! We think he killed Miss Mitchell and he's going to kill us too!"

Mrs. Williams did not look as shocked as Lizzie expected her to. Instead, her hands that were usually so carefully manicured but which now had dirty and broken fingernails were peeling Lizzie's fingers one by one from around her neck as she answered,

"Alright, calm down. I know all about it. It seems you three have been causing us some problems."

She peered over the top of her gild-rimmed glasses at them, scowling as if they had been caught cheating in an exam. It took ages for Lizzie to understand what her favourite teacher was saying. When she did her legs turned to jelly and she put her hands out to steady herself as the walls around her began to spin.

"You're one of them too!" Tom gasped. "It was you behind us on the bank just now!"

"Yes you're quite right Tom, well done," the woman replied. "Teaching doesn't pay well you know," she said as if she needed to explain her actions. "I've had to do lots of other jobs to live the way I want."

"Dad always did wonder how you could afford a jag," Tom mumbled in disgust, referring to the car that Oliver had damaged.

Mrs. Williams spun round to face him, "Just watch what you say young man. I've worked hard to get where I am and little thanks I get for it."

She dropped her voice and although she was only short Tom shrank away from her as she said, "I deserve more than I get for running this place!"

Suddenly she stepped back and the moment of danger passed. "Well now," she said. "I want you to think of this as a steep learning curve. You're about to learn what happens when you interfere with things that don't concern you. I think George should be ready for us by now so let's go and join him shall we?"

Before the children could argue or even collect their thoughts she had pulled Oliver to his feet and was bustling along the corridor with them towards the gym changing rooms.

There "George" or P.C. Pane as the children knew him, was waiting. His large buttocks perched uncomfortably on a narrow bench that was designed for much smaller bottoms. At his feet lay lengths of coiled nylon cord and the heavy weights that went with the exercise benches the men's community group used in the evenings.

He stood up quickly when they entered but did not look at the children. He seemed to have lost his earlier aggressive manner and he stood like an awkward schoolboy with his hands in his pockets. There was no sign of the gun now.

"Look," he started to say, "I'm not sure I can go through with this."

"Oh! For goodness sake! Don't you get soft on me too! You know what happens to people when they do that. You know what happened to Fiona Mitchell! Stupid woman! She brought all those ridiculous foreigners over just because she felt sorry for them! What did she think I was going to do with them all? Find them all jobs in the school canteen? If I could kill her with just a candlestick I'm sure I can deal with you now I've got the gun."

The head teacher patted her pocket as she spoke. "You should have sorted these wretched urchins out long ago when it would have been blamed on the Albanians. Now we've got to make it look like an accident, a childish prank gone wrong. It'll look like they broke in and were playing about in here. They've been breaking in to places all holiday, nobody'll suspect a thing. You know what has to be done, get on with it!"

The policeman did as he was told and held out a five-kilo weight to the children who each took one. Then quickly and deftly he tied the nylon cord round them passing the rope through the centre of every weight until they were trussed and bunched together like a bouquet of flowers.

Whether they didn't struggle because everything happened so quickly, or because they were so used to behaving themselves for Mrs. Williams in school, Lizzie didn't know. But none of the children made any attempt to stop what was going on, even though they had every reason to suspect and fear the worst.

Sure enough, the next thing they knew the two adults were pulling and pushing them out of the changing rooms and through into the swimming pool area. The smell of the chlorine took Lizzie's breath away before they were even near the water and she looked towards Oliver to see his reaction. The chemical always made his eyes sting and he couldn't stay in a swimming pool for longer than ten minutes at a time.

Seeing the look on her brother's face made tears well up in her eyes as Lizzie realized that the chlorine was the least of his problems.

At last, too late, as they reached the edge of the pool Tom started to struggle. He screamed in rage at the killers using language his two young friends had never heard before. He kicked out at the adults' legs, but he was too well bound and his efforts were useless.

The two people, who the children should have been able to trust with their lives, pulled the youngsters down to the deep end of the pool and launched them off the side into the cold, blue water.

Tom carried on struggling, frantically trying to reach the cord's knot that was tied behind his back. But it was impossible. Tied together as they were and with the weights dragging them under they had no chance of staying above the water.

The only thing Lizzie could do now was make what was about to happen as easy for Oliver as possible. It was, after all, her fault. Once again she wished she hadn't got them involved in this in the first place. With her last gulp of air she cried, "Oliver, you know I love you."

"I know," Oliver answered, spitting water out of his mouth. Strangely, the last thing Lizzie thought she heard him say as her head went under the water was, "You love dogs too."

Just as she was giving way to the blackness that was swallowing her Lizzie heard crashing and banging noises, as if doors were being smashed back on their hinges. Then what sounded like barking!

Suddenly she was sucking in great gulps of sweet, fresh air at the same time as something wet and warm was smothering her face.

She heard a deep, gentle voice say, "Come on little Miss, don't let go." Opening her eyes she saw a huge white dog in front of her, licking the water off her face with its tongue. Big Bear was cradling her and the other two children in his arms, while with his knife his brother was slashing the cords that tied them.

"How did you get here?" she asked looking into the man's kind grey eyes.

"You called us. Well... you called my dog," Big Bear answered, holding up Oliver's mysterious object.

When she looked puzzled the man put it to his lips and blew and his dog pricked up its ears and tilted its head to one side.

"Oh" said Tom. "It's a silent dog whistle."

At that moment they became aware of movement from the other side of the water and they looked over to where Mrs. Williams and P.C. Pane were running down the edge of the swimming pool making for the door at the far end.

Big Bear gave a command that only the dog understood and immediately it leapt to its feet and raced after the fleeing pair. They stopped at the end of the pool, their exit barred by the ferocious looking beast that stood in front of them, teeth bared, growling.

The dog took a step forward, the policeman took a step back teetering on the curved edging slab. He tried to regain his balance and clutched out wildly at the air grabbing a handful of Mrs. Williams's short, dark curly hair. Toppling backwards he fell into the water taking the shrieking head teacher with him.

The two Albanian men and their dog stayed guard over their captives as they floundered in the water, at the same time comforting the children until the police arrived.

As they were bundled into separate police cars Big Bear winked at Lizzie and called out to her "I have left you a gift in your jungle."

*

That evening, after the children had once again been thoroughly checked over by Dr Bell, they led their parents on a slow procession down to their den.

Peering through the twilight gloom they spotted a bundle of rags lying in one corner. As Lizzie started to unwrap the roll of material it wriggled, then yelped.

The folds of cloth dropped open and out popped two little snow white heads and two pairs of doggy eyes blinked sleepily at the delighted girl!

It didn't take long for the whole story to emerge. The three pillars of society; the vicar, the policeman and the teacher were smuggling human cargo into Britain from Albania. The vicar thought she was helping people, but the other two were only doing it for the money.

Despite their poverty the illegal immigrants had each paid thousands of pounds for the chance to start a new life in a new country.

Because of their bravery and selflessness in saving the youngsters the Home Office decided that Big Bear and his brother could stay in Britain. A local businessman rewarded their courage by offering them employment and they and their families settled down quite close to Allsworthy village.

Williams and Pane were tried at the Old Bailey in London and cheers rang out in the courtroom and the village pub when they were found guilty and sent to prison for life.

Leicestershire Police force gave Lizzie, Tom and Oliver medals for bravery. Oliver keeps his on his bedroom windowsill next to his very dusty collection of dead spiders.

And Lizzie's mum agreed that the puppies could stay. "They're so cute," she said. "How much trouble can they be?"

Oliver began to tell her, "Actually, Pyrenees Mountain dogs need a lot of looking after…."

Together Lizzie and Tom shouted,

"Shut up Oliver!"

Kingdom by
d., Milton Keynes